GW00500681

For Andy, my dear brother, whose insatiable
appetite for my work has spurred me forward.

THE SKULLS OF LUBAANTUN

Book 1 of the Ortec Saga

R.J. Flux

PublishAmerica
Baltimore

First printing

ISBN: 1-4137-6152-6
PUBLISHED BY PUBLISHAMERICA, LLLP
www.publishamerica.com
Baltimore

Printed in the United States of America

Chapter 1
The Dividing of the Skulls

Far above the hills, the sun shone down in a cloudless sky.

In the distance, the monotonous drone of chanting could be heard from the altar temple at the heart of the Mayan City complex.

It was mid morning and already, the city's inhabitants had congregated upon the top of the temple to witness the last ceremony of the skulls.

The shaman stood at the head of the stone lectern in full ceremonial garb, surveying the turnout through half-closed eyes.

With a capricious wave of his hand, the chanting ceased and all eyes were upon him.

"Today," he began. "Today we worship the skulls for the last time. This is not the end, but the beginning of a new era for our people." He raised the ceremonial staff aloft and an almighty cheer went up from the crowded courtyard.

"The skulls have afforded us protection and good harvests since they were sent to us by the sun god, Inti. But now they must be returned." There were a few murmurs of doubt in the crowd and the shaman sensed this.

"Fear not, people. We are a great civilization who have been and will continue to be great. Inti sees that we are great and wishes us to prove that from her guidance, we have learnt to flourish and spread throughout the land on our own."

The confused faces within the crowd soon disappeared, and the shaman knew his job was done.

"At first light tomorrow, we will take the skulls to the temple of Venus and pay homage to Inti for her guidance. There the skulls will be returned to their place among the stars."

That night many people didn't sleep for they knew that the next day would be a celebration. A celebration of independence and freedom form the nursery-like hold of the skulls. The city eventually fell silent, apart from one individual shadow that crept through the thin, perpendicular streets towards the temple steps.

The thin, wiry figure crept up the steps in absolute silence towards the large, thickset doors that lead inside the temple.

The guards were dozing at their posts and neither of them even heard a whisper as the figure slid silently by them and in through the doors to the chamber where the skulls were housed.

Once inside, the figure stepped into the subtle glow of the torches within the main passage and removed the llama-skin robe that obscured her features.

The light cast down upon a young woman with tanned, smooth skin and short straight hair. She held in her left hand a small silver blade, and in the right a peculiar crescent-shaped pendant.

She gingerly stepped through the door at the end of the passage into the chamber of skulls, and gazed in awe at the spectacle that she beheld.

In the center of the room was a huge stone pedestal, upon which sat an even bigger stone dais covered with ornate Mayan scripture and pictograms.

Set around the rim of the dais were thirteen polished sockets large enough to accommodate a human head or a...

The door behind her slammed with a heart-stopping thud. She spun around, dagger poised to strike, but there was nothing to strike at.

She gave a little sigh and turned back to the dais, only to be confronted and then grabbed by an apparition in silver and black clothing and a highly polished faceplate obscuring its features.

A second pair of hands suddenly grabbed her. She tried to crane her head around to see but she was unable, held by some invisible force other than that of her immediate captor.

Suddenly, her head was thrown back and a blinding, all encompassing light flooded down on her from above. There was a sharp popping sound and then, as suddenly as it had begun, the light vanished and she was left on the floor of the chamber in complete darkness. She wanted to cry out, but as much as tried she could make no sound. Inside her head, she screamed with fear. As exhaustion and trauma took hold, she slipped into the spinning oblivion that was unconsciousness.

She became aware of consciousness returning before she opened her eyes.

Far off in the distance, she heard voices. Angry voices shouting at her.

A pair of hands was felt grabbing at her arms and immediately she was awake, trying to fight off her assailant.

She snapped open her eyes, and shut them immediately. "The light, keep the light away!" she was saying, over and over. She felt the hands release her and she passed out again.

When she awoke for the second time, there was very little light around.

Was it evening or had some of the torches been extinguished in the chamber?

Then she realized she was no longer in the chamber. Instead, she was in a soft bed in a small room with high windows.

She sat bolt upright, and at the rustle of her motion, a figure, who she had failed to notice in the far left corner of the room, got up and proceed to move towards her, saying in a soft voice, "You're safe now. Don't be afraid."

She tried to focus in the diminishing light. "Where am I?"

The figure sat at the foot of the bed. "You're in my house. I am Kaitan, the city healer."

He put out his hand to feel her brow. She instinctively backed away. "It's alright, child. I will not harm you." He placed his hand upon her forehead and gave himself a satisfactory grunt. "Your fever has passed." She managed to focus properly, and for the first time since she had awoken, managed to get a good look at her apparent savior.

He was an elderly man with a thin, white beard and close-set eyes. His hair lay straight against the sides of his head and flowed over his shoulders. She noticed that he walked with the aid of a staff. Initially, she thought that this would make for an easy escape, but then she noticed that the door had been barricaded from the inside.

"Wha...what happened to me?"

The old man gave her a puzzled look. "You don't remember, do you?" He proceeded to tell her that the alarm had been raised in the early hours of the morning and that someone had broken into the sacred chamber of skulls and stolen them. She had been found unconscious on the floor with the peculiar pendant. The guards and the shaman had tried to interrogate her, but had met with no success.

She had been taken to the shaman's house under guard, when in a frenzy of rage she had lashed out at one of the guards and had startled them, so lethargic had been her appearance, and had made her getaway down the back streets until she had collapsed in a doorway opposite to the healer's.

"I heard the commotion outside and went to see what was going on. I saw you and felt unable to leave you there. I have barricaded the door because I noticed by your facial tattoos that you are not from this city." He gave her and inquisitive eye. "And now you are being hunted down by the temple guards as the 'thief of the skulls.'"

She went to swing herself out of bed and yelped as she felt the searing hot sensation of pain shoot down her left side. She instinctively cupped her hand over what she thought was a stab wound that she may have received while escaping from the guards, but as she touched it she drew her hand away quickly. It was icy cold. "I have examined the wound, but am unable to treat it. It has been made by no weapon I am familiar with," Kaitan told her.

She looked down at her side and noticed a large, dark, triangular burn just bellow her ribs. She gasped slightly at the sight of such a bizarre mark.

"What is your name, my dear?"

She looked a little bewildered at the question. "Chiuna," she answered after a short pause. "I have not stolen any skulls!" she added abruptly.

"What is the reason for your presence in this city?" Kaitan asked after a while.

She gave him a shameful glance.

"I...I was sent here by my chieftain to steal your Chulel because our crops are failing and our people are dying."

At that, she began to feel around her person frantically.

"Are you looking for this, my dear?" asked Kaitan, and he held up the strange pendant.

"Give me that!" she demanded.

Kaitan snatched it away from her.

"I will return this to you when you tell me what you were really doing in the temple and what you know of the disappearance of the skulls."

Her eyes widened with anger. "I don't know anything about any skulls!" she shouted back at him. She took a few deep breaths and proceeded to tell him what she remembered of her ordeal in the temple and of the strangely dressed assailant who had held her in that awful light. Kaitan recoiled in horror as she described these events in detail.

"No, no, this cannot be. You're lying. They dare not return. Not now!" he said. "I must inform the shaman at once. You should stay here. If you're seen in the city complex, you'll be killed on sight." She looked up at him.

"Why are you doing this, old man?" she asked.

"I'll explain later. Right now stay here and do not open the door to anyone until I return. I will explain all then."

She lay back on the bed and tried to relax despite the pain that she was in. She heard the scuffing and creaking of furniture as Kaitan cleared the door, then she heard the door creak open and it close with a solid thud.

Far above the city complex, the shaman stood at the alter stone and tried to understand why the stranger had come in the middle of the night and how she had made off with all thirteen skulls, but was not in possession of them when she was captured.

"Shaman." He turned to see one of the king's servants standing a few feet away.

"Yes, what is it?"

"The king wishes to see you immediately, sir."

He turned and walked towards the king's chambers. Inside, the king sat on his throne, surrounded by his attendants and his daughter. The shaman walked to the foot of the throne and knelt down and bowed his head.

"Shaman," the king began. "What is to be done to recover the skulls?" The shaman opened his mouth to speak, but the king began again "You are aware that if the skulls are not taken to the temple of Venus by the end of the season, Great Inti will retake the Chulel, and rain famine and pestilence down upon us for not fulfilling her wishes." He was about to speak again when one of the guards came running in to the chamber.

"Your highness, the healer wishes an audience with you."

The king looked a little bemused

"What does he want, guard?" asked to shaman sharply.

"He claims to have knowledge of the skulls, sire."

The king leaned forward on the arms of the throne. "Show him in, quickly."

The guard scurried out of the chamber and reappeared a few moments later with Kaitan in tow. The healer hobbled towards the throne.

"King Chuuta, I bring news of the skulls."

The king ordered one of his attendants to bring a stool for Kaitan to sit on. He could see the old man was exhausted from rushing here.

"What is your news, healer?" the king asked inquisitively.

Kaitan sat on the stool and leaned on his staff to catch his breath.

"Sire, they've returned."

The shaman folded his arms and sighed. "Who have?" asked the king. Kaitan shuddered as he spoke.

"It is the demons of fire and darkness, my king!" The king physically shook with rage and fear. He stood up and turned to the attendant who stood to the left of him.

"Situan, bring me my battle headdress. I must address the people."

He turned back to Kaitan. The old man was fairly exhausted from his ordeal.

"See that the healer is returned safely to his home and compensated for his troubles."

Kaitan, still seated, bowed slightly in respect of the king's gracefulness. The shaman darted to the king's side.

"Your highness, may I inquire as to your plans concerning this incident." The king looked the shaman in the face.

"Sound the gathering horn. We will need everyone in the city to be in the courtyard within one hour. We will not allow these mischievous demons to jeopardize the future of this great city." The shaman looked a little disheveled at being ordered to perform what he considered to be a menial task but did as he was bade.

Within the hour, the courtyard was alive with noisy, confused residents who were anxious to know the fate concerning the skulls and what their king proposed to do to regain them.

The king strode out onto the balcony high above the courtyard and looked down onto the packed square filled with his subjects. After he had approached the edge, he heard the sounds of two thousand voices fade away rapidly and anxious faces turned upward towards him.

He took a deep breath, raised his arms and began.

"Citizens, you are aware of the peril that faces us. We must act now to avert disaster and plague raining down upon us."

The king's aide came up behind him and placed the ceremonial battle helmet upon his head and handed him the golden scepter which he held aloft.

"I will take one man from each family to join the ranks of the guard to go in search and retrieve the skulls. We will destroy the demons and retake what is ours!"

A cheer went up from the crowd as the king raised his arms triumphantly in a gesture of victory.

As the troops began to amass in the central courtyard, the cheering was becoming almost deafening. Cries of admiration were being shouted by young and old alike while the wives and mothers of the men were busy fussing over them with tear-filled eyes, muttering prayers of hope and safe return.

The shaman stood at the top of the great stone steps, arms raised in victory.

It hadn't occurred to him that the cheering was rapidly dying away until almost silence fell. He looked down at the bemused and somewhat frightened faces about him. At first he thought that all eyes were on him, but then he realized that they were actually looking past him to the sky above.

The shaman craned his neck up behind him to see what had caused the sudden silence to befall the crowd. At first the sun was in his eyes, but as he squinted he noticed that from behind one of the wispy white, strafe-like clouds, a dark, wedge-shaped object was swooping around the plateau in a wide, lazy arc. At first he took it for one of the great condors, the huge sacred birds that inhabited this mountain region, but as the shape grew nearer, a low buzzing sound was becoming audible.

Before he knew what was happening, the object had shot from its original arc-like path and was descending rapidly towards the complex. There was total silence as the crowd below watched with amazed curiosity as this strange, wedged-shaped harbinger grew larger and larger as it descended. Without warning, the black wedge plummeted in a direct line towards the crowd and began raining fire upon them. The humming grew louder and explosions were erupting all over the complex. The crowd scattered, screaming and running in all directions. The blasts were precise and the people were being picked off one by one.

Larger explosions took out whole groups running in all directions.

While this aerial massacre taking place, the shaman stood at the top of the steps, his arms still outstretched, with tears streaming down his face.

He suddenly came to his senses and began chanting curses and ritual spells to dispel this great flying, fire belching monster.

He stopped in mid chant. The monster had swung out of a second dive and now hovered, motionless, above the courtyard. It just hung there, glaring at him, its nostrils still releasing thin streamers of smoke. The anger welled up inside the shaman. He thought he was going to explode. Behind him, the doors of the king's chamber swung open and the king, his daughter and at least three guards rushed out, evidently alarmed at the commotion. They all stopped dead in their tracks at the sight of the black, smooth, wedge-shaped tormentor that hung there glaring at them with its one illuminated, pulsing eye.

Without warning, the monster belched forth its all-consuming fire, and the entire temple and its occupants were vaporized.

After the almost complete eradication of the inhabitants, the wedge slowly began to rise, but halfway through its ascent, it stopped, spun around and evidently took a great deal of notice of the lone survivor who was frantically clambering over the still-smoldering rubble. This individual wore a llama skin cloak, and in her hand was a bizarre crescent-shaped pendant.

The wedge moved slowly to intercept her. As it hovered barely thirty feet above her, the same constricting feeling rushed over her and the blinding white light was back. There was a loud pop; a flicker of red, and the girl had vanished.

With this event over, the wedge slowly ascended and moved toward the mountain. Upon the summit, this strange craft proceeded to repeat the lurid light show, and after a few seconds, it completed its task and shot skywards so fast, it left a sonic boom in its wake. Not that there was anyone around to hear it.

As it rose, it released a tiny sphere, which plummeted earthwards with no more effort than a stone flung from a cliff. Only this was no stone. Upon striking the ground, it created an encompassing expanding ball of light that blasted outwards, leaving a huge mushroom-shaped plume of fire at its center. The flash lasted only a second or so, but after that second had passed, not a single trace of civilization was left. It was as if the temple complex and its thousands of inhabitants had never existed.

The wedge finally passed out of Earth's cloudy atmosphere into the cold void of space where it stopped dead.

Facing it was an enormous silver, cigar-shaped craft. The wedge let forth a full volley of fire at it and veered off at a sharp right turn. The cigar craft, completely unscathed by the attack, turned around towards its fleeing assailant and emitted a single green beam. The shot hit home, and the wedge-shaped craft exploded with incandescent fury, scattering its flaming remnants throughout Earth's atmosphere. Then, turning lazily towards the stars, the cigar-shaped craft returned from whence it came.

The remnants of the wedge craft seemed to burn up harmlessly in the atmosphere, but as it incinerated in the white hot friction, thirteen tiny, blazing fragments shot off in all directions and descended back to the planet's surface in a broad, chaotic star formation.

The skulls had returned once more to the Earth.

Chapter 2
A Profound Discovery

She stood up and stretched her limbs. The effects from being exposed to the blazing heat of the noon sun had made her feel very dirty, and the telltale signs of excessive sweat under her arms and down her back and chest signified that she had been out in this heat for some time.

The excavating brush that she held in her hand was caked in fine, light brown soil. It had been a very long morning.

She gave a frustrated sigh and was about to bend down and resume her laborious task when she heard a voice call her name.

"Belinda! Belinda!"

She turned and squinted down the plateau in the direction of the voice.

A short, rotund man was calling to her from the encampment some fifty feet below her. Belinda Osborne was an archaeologist with a flair for the abnormal.

She put down the brush and walked down the low hill toward the fat man. She pulled a dirty white handkerchief from her pocket and wiped her dusty face as she walked.

The fat man waiting for her was Karl Weston, an overfed, alabaster white product of excessive indulgence and a convenient city lifestyle who had about as much knowledge of archaeology as a goldfish did about astronomy.

He was, however, the sole investor who was funding the dig and had insisted that he see, firsthand, how his well-invested funds were being spent.

Belinda chuckled to herself as she approached him. He looked like something straight out of a tacky 1960s murder mystery with his dusty white linen suit and his crumpled Panama hat that sat at a slightly jaunty angle on his short black shock of hair.

He seemed excited, but Belinda couldn't be sure if it was the little man's glee or the heat that had turned his rubicund features redder than normal.

"Belinda, you must see this, my dear! One of the diggers has uncovered a skeleton!"

She walked straight past him and headed for the water butt.

"In a minute, Karl, I'm dry as a bone here."

Belinda ladled some water to her mouth. It was quite warm but it quenched her thirst nonetheless.

"Come along, Belinda! This is important. Hurry up!"

Belinda rolled her eyes as she tied her dusty brown hair back into a ponytail.

"OK, OK, I'm coming."

After she had adjusted herself, she followed Karl down from the camp to the cool shade at the foot of the plateau. He seemed to skip lightly as he waddled off ahead of her.

Like a kid at Christmas, she thought to herself.

Karl wasn't an odious man, but he really knew how get on someone's nerves when the mood took him, but Belinda remembered that it was his money that was keeping them all in a job.

As they approached the dig site, Belinda realized that there was something out of the ordinary. At least thirty people had crowded around the point that Karl was excitedly bustling towards. "Everyone's seen skeletons before." Belinda thought to herself.

This level of activity was evidently unusual to say the least. She heard Karl asking people to kindly move aside in his squeaky little voice. When she was barely ten feet from the crowd, she saw Karl give a whoop of glee and a little jump.

"Give me some room please. Come on guys, you've all seen a skele—"

Belinda's sentence ended abruptly as she bent over and stared down at the carefully excavated remains that lay before her.

"See, my dear! I told you it was exciting, didn't I!"

Belinda gave a little scoff.

"Is this some kind of sick joke? I mean come on, guys. We've got some serious work to do here, and it doesn't help matters any if you lot are playing pranks."

"Belinda, this is no hoax!" Tito Fernandez, one of Belinda's long time dig partners had now left his place in the tight crowd and made his way around to where Belinda stood with her hands on her hips and a disdained look on her face. Belinda gave a sidelong look and then bent back down over the recently excavated remains. The group instinctively moved back almost as if she had asked them to do so telepathically.

Now the sun cast its light over the excavations, eliminating the shadows of the group that had dispersed from the rim of the pit. Belinda's face changed from one of disbelief to excitement. There in the shallow pit before her, lay the skeletal remains of a man, a man with four arms.

She took up a brush and gently but slightly frantically proceeded to sweep away the excess dirt from around the shoulder joints, evidently in an attempt to see if there were any signs of tampering with the remains to make this hoax creature. After all, the guys had played pranks on her before.

Belinda found none. If this truly was a genuine skeleton, then in life it would have stood some seven feet tall, had an extremely large stride, and, of course, it had four upper limbs tapering down to four broad hands and seven slender fingers.

Karl began squeaking with delight as he watched Belinda's face confirm that this was no hoax. Belinda shot him a sidelong glance then turned to Tito.

"Tito, get this thing out of the earth and into the tent for examination. I want every test done...*twice*. Karl, a word, please."

Belinda almost dragged Karl away from the edge of the pit and into his tent.

"Did you know about this? Is this the reason you were so eager to fund my team?"

Karl looked a little crestfallen.

"Belinda, I funded your work because personally I find archeology a fascinating topic. All my associates buy themselves condominiums and fast cars. I on the other hand like to, ahem, get my hands dirty."

He stood there in his ridiculously expensive white suit and dusty Panama hat, beaming like some grossly overweight cherub.

Despite all her misgivings, Belinda always found it hard to stay mad at Karl. She had worked for an old friend of Karl's some years ago and that was when they first met. Even on that first meeting, Belinda warmed to him. He had given Belinda her first financial "helping hand" when she had been turned down for an archeology grant from the University of Schenectady in New York.

Karl had believed in her when all others had given her the brush off.

"And besides, I thought we might find something of interest out here."

Belinda looked slightly puzzled. She was fully aware that Karl possessed very little knowledge of archeology, and this prompted suspicion in her. Karl turned away from her and bustled over to his packing cases, which stood in the corner of his tent.

He fumbled about in his pocket for a few moments and then produced a small bunch of keys with which he unlocked the topmost case in the stack. Belinda couldn't quite see what he had but he was evidently being very careful with it. A few moments later, he returned to her holding an ebony box with a large brass latch.

"This was the reason I wanted you out here, Belinda. I picked this up at my conservative club from a friend of a friend. It was found a few miles from here and I wanted your expert opinion on it. I must stress, however," Karl's face was suddenly stony and his voice had taken on a flat, serious tone, "you must not tell anyone about what you are about to see."

He set the box on a small table that stood in the corner, unlocked the latch and opened it.

He lifted out the contents and turned to Belinda; what she saw made her jaw drop.

A small smirk spread across Karl's face. In his hands sat the most perfectly formed human skull Belinda had ever seen. This skull, however, was of purest jade. The tiny rods of sunlight that pierced the vents in the canvas roof hit the skull and sent an emerald light show cascading throughout the tent.

Belinda stood there dumbstruck, in absolute awe of what Karl now held in his hands. Her eyes flicked from the skull to Karl and back to the skull again

"Wha...what is it?" she said in a hushed voice. Karl's benign, cherubim expression had returned.

"It's one of the skulls from the lost city of Lubaantun, my dear!" he said with an excited squeak. He held out the skull for Belinda. She gingerly stepped forward and took the skull in both hands with the gentleness of holding a newborn baby. The skull was lighter than she thought it would be. Its emerald facets winked and sparkled at her in the shafts of light, and she fancied that she could see something embedded at its center, something very small and spherical.

"What are the skulls of Lubaantun?" she asked as she handed the skull back to Karl, who took it with the same due care.

"Legend has it that Lubaantun was once the greatest city in the Mayan empire and its ruins are reported to be on this very plateau. However, no remains have ever been found, until now."

He replaced the skull in its case and locked it securely, then turned back to Belinda and leaned against one of the packing cases in a manner that made him appear more rotund than usual.

"Some schools of thought believe that there are ancient scriptures that tell of the legend of the skulls. There are believed to be thirteen in total, each one made from a different mineral or precious stone." He paused to allow Belinda to digest this piece of information.

"That still doesn't explain that 'spiderman' out there." She folded her arms that denoted that now he had told her this much, there was no way she was going to let him stop now.

"Oh that!" Karl said with a smirk. "That's an alien."

The sentence rolled from his tongue as if to say something like this was an everyday occurrence. Belinda scoffed slightly.

"I was beginning to wonder when we were going to get to little green space men," she said with utter disdain.

Karl gave a little sigh.

"Belinda, what do you think that skull is made from? Hum?"

She was beginning to look a little peeved.

"Jade or emerald I suppose."

Karl began to beam like a Cheshire cat.

"WRONG!" he almost sung. "I had some of the best geologists in the world have a look at this thing, privately I might add. Don't want to attract any unwanted attention now, do we? Every one of them came back with same results. They all told me that the mineral or gem that this thing is made from does not exist in any modern or indeed, ancient, geological element table. Every test came back 'substance unknown.'"

By this time the sun had began to slowly continue it path across the western sky and the air was beginning to cool.

"I don't know about you, but I could kill for a cold beer," said Belinda as she stretched her arms above her head.

"Capital idea. I'll join you in a few moments," said Karl.

Belinda left the tent into the late afternoon sun, leaving Karl to bustle busily in the tent, no doubt securing the skull back into its place in the teetering tower of crates in the corner of the tent. Belinda made her way over to the huge awning that was set up in the middle of their shanty town of tents where Tito and the rest of the team were busy examining the remains of the "alien" that had been mysteriously uncovered up on this lonely plateau.

"Anything interesting, Tito?" said Belinda as she approached the examination table. Tito turned to her, holding his hands up, surgeon style. The latex gloves that he wore were flecked with dots of blue liquid. "You-a not gonna believes this, Belinda!" he said. Apparently Karl's childlike attitude to new discoveries was contagious. Tito was bobbing from foot to foot, grinning from ear to ear. "This-a stuff has comma outta the bones!"

"What?" she said, as she shot forward past him to the table, barging one or two of the others out of the way in the process. Sure enough, on the table was the skeleton, and exuding from its dry, dirt-crusted joints were thin trickles of a viscous blue liquid.

"This day is just getting weirder and weirder!"

Tito was chuckling to himself as she scanned the remains from feet to skull.

"Get a sample of this and…"

Tito interceded, "Anda put in ona ice for a DNA analysis, no questions asked?" He grinned broadly at her. "Anda I already told everybody that they say nada about any o' this! Okay?"

She smiled at him. "What would I do without you?"

He smiled back at her. "Whatta indeed," he said.

Belinda let them continue with their work while she took a look at some of the photos they had taken when they first brought the skeleton up to be examined. She paid particular attention to one of the creature's skull. She had seen this shaped head numerous times before in magazines or on the TV, but at the moment, she couldn't place it. Tracing her finger across the glossy surface, following the contours of the heavy brow bone, the sloping nasal cavities and elongated audio cavities and the flat, broad forehead gave the skull a tapered almost square appearance.

Karl came waddling up to the awning, wheezing slightly.

"Are you ready for that drink, Belinda?" he panted. She acknowledged him and they walked from the awning and headed for the canteen tent together.

That evening as the rest of the team had either gone home or settled down in their tents, Karl and Belinda sat out in front of his tent drinking expensive bourbon, and Karl blew clouds of blue smoke from a fat Havana cigar.

"Where do you think they came from Karl?" Belinda asked, looking up at the cloudless, star-strewn sky.

"Sorry?" he replied.

"So, these aliens, where do you think they came from?"

Karl looked a little surprised. "You've changed your tune, my dear."

Belinda gave him a thin smile. "Well, let's be honest. It's not every day you come across something like this, is it? I mean I usually spend my time digging up and dusting off the bones of dinosaurs or the occasional Pliocene ape."

Karl stubbed out the last remnants of his cigar on a nearby stone and swigged back the rest of his bourbon.

"I have a friend coming up to see us tomorrow. He's a biologist...of sorts; studies alien remains and artifacts as a bit of a hobby, and has been trying to prove the existence of extraterrestrials for years!"

Belinda looked a bit uneasy about letting yet another person in on their discovery.

"He's a bit eccentric, mind you, but I think he may be able to give us some answers as to the origins of our multi-limbed friend."

There was one thing that had been puzzling Belinda ever since Karl had shown her the skull earlier that day.

"Karl. How the hell have you managed to keep a lid on this all this time? I mean, normally, this place would have been crawling with government scientists and the military. How come it's just us?"

Karl struggled to his feet and wandered back into the tent to fetch another bottle of bourbon. As he came out again, He was beaming like a mischievous child.

"There are some advantages to being wealthy, you know. The Peruvian government has been extremely cooperative ever since I left a generous donation to them for the autonomous rights to this plateau. Not to mention, they agreed to deny all knowledge of our presence up here." Belinda looked completely taken aback.

"Karl Weston," she began in a tone of an annoyed headmistress, "you get me and my team up here on false pretenses, bribe an entire government, and get them to lie to their foreign counterparts if they show an interest in this area! And there's me thinking you were a pillar of the community!"

She raised her glass as Karl offered to pour her out another measure of the dark brown bourbon.

He raised his glass to the heavens. "A toast to a profound discovery!" exclaimed Karl.

They chinked their glasses together and sunk the last of the bourbon before Belinda got up, wished Karl a good night and walked back to her tent with a slightly lightheaded feeling.

The bourbon, if anything, would help her sleep tonight, because with all that had happened today, sleep was the last thing on her mind.

The Second Skull
Chapter 3

The next morning, Belinda awoke to the sounds of raised voices outside. Somewhere near the awning, she judged. She rose and dressed quickly, and after leaving her tent, she saw up the rise Karl, still dressed in his nightclothes, keeping two of the local laborers at bay with a sun umbrella. Belinda sprinted up to them.

"Karl, what's going on here?" Karl half turned to her, still keeping one eye fixed on the two young men who, judging by their faces, were obviously afraid of something.

"I caught these two trying to leave with some of our supplies. They've been babbling some gibberish and nonsense since I caught them!"

He stood there, wheezing heavily and brandishing the parasol like a swashbuckling walrus. Belinda turned to the two young men. They definitely seemed spooked over something. Walking past Karl, Belinda strode right up to the two men and asked them outright in their native tongue why they were so desperate to take supplies and depart, posthaste.

They frantically recited what they had evidently tried to tell Karl. One of them began to weep. Belinda turned to Karl and said, "They're afraid of the skull and what they believe it can do." Karl stood up straight and tried to compose himself.

"Rubbish!" he said hotly. "You and I are the only two people who know that I possess the skull, let alone laid eyes upon it!"

Belinda turned back to the two men, who were both now on they're knees. The one who had been weeping was now mumbling to himself. She asked them how they knew of the skull and they replied with the same frantic response. At this, she must have told them to return to their tent and stay there. Grudgingly and shaking somewhat, they seemed to reluctantly agree and scurried off down the rise to the encampment. Belinda spun around to where Karl was now propping himself up on the parasol, Chaplin-style.

"They know about the skull, Karl, because they've *seen* it!" Karl gasped and almost lost his balance.

"Impossible!" he retorted. "The skull is under my bed. I put it there before I went to sleep last night. Come on, I'll show you!" They both made they're way back to Karl's tent and once inside, he proceeded to remove the same dark wooden box from which Belinda had first seen the skull. Karl placed it on the bed and opened it so that the cover was facing Belinda. He lifted the cover off completely and smiled smugly at her. He, of course, standing with the back of the box facing him could not see the content. Belinda sighed, leaned over the box and picked up a large lump of sandstone. Karl squealed with anger. Someone during the night had crept into his tent and stolen the skull, but to add insult to injury, the thief had taken the liberty to replace it with the sandstone that Belinda now held in her hands.

"The bastard who did this is going to swing from the gallows!!" Belinda was shocked. Despite the situation, she had never heard Karl talk so colorfully or aggressively about another human being.

"Well. We now know how those two men saw the skull. The question is who stole it?"

They both agreed not to say anything concerning the theft simply because up to now, no one knew about the skull. Belinda decided she was hungry, and after explaining that on her way up here, she came past the vehicles and they were all there, she left for the canteen. At hearing this, Karl relaxed ever so slightly and he also decided that he could function better on a full stomach. He hurriedly dressed and barreled down the rise after her. Belinda explained that if none of the vehicles were missing, then the thief had either left by foot or they were still here. Upon arriving at the canteen, they both saw every member of the team sat around the trestle tables, tucking into breakfast. Even the two frightened laborers were there, sitting in a corner not looking or talking to anyone.

"I'll handle this!" said Karl, and without even looking at Belinda he puffed himself up, pushed his hat slightly forward and marched up to the breakfasters.

"Ladies and gentlemen, may I have your attention please! We have a thief in our midst. I want a full tent inspection in ten minutes! Every last item is to be laid out in front of your tents and there will be no arguments. I am the one funding this excavation and also the one paying your wages. Anyone who does not comply will NOT get paid and will be expelled from the site, *immediately*!"

There was a unanimous groan of displeasure from the group, but they seemed to understand as Karl's speech was translated hurriedly into about three different languages. Within two minutes of his departure from the canteen, there was an exodus of people heading in all directions back to their tents. Karl strode back up to Belinda, beaming with pride.

"As they say, money talks, my dear!"

Belinda couldn't believe her ears. She had really learned a lot about Karl Weston these last few days.

"Quite the born leader, aren't you, Karl?" she said with just a hint of admiration. Sure enough, within ten minutes or so, all the tents in the camp had their contents haphazardly strewn out in front of them. Karl inspected the tents on the left side of the camp, and Belinda, the right. It wasn't until she had almost finished looking through the combined possessions of ten tents when she realized that she hadn't seen Tito all morning. The thought that he could be the thief flashed in her brain for a split second, but she dismissed it just as quickly. As she pondered over the possible whereabouts of the skull, she caught sight of something out of the corner of her eye. Just over the rise where she had parted Karl and the two laborers, she noticed that there were two round black shapes bobbing up and down, but then she realized that they were the heads of two people approaching the top of the rise from the other side. The sun was in her eyes so it made it very difficult to distinguish who there people were. Just then, Karl came waddling up beside her

"Who the devil are they?" he inquired.

Belinda brought her hand up over her eyes in an attempt to see better

"It's Tito!" she said as Karl followed suit for a better look.

"Oh good, he's found Neville!" said Karl. Belinda turned to Karl and lowered her hand. "Who's Neville? Oh, is he the scientist you were talking about yesterday?"

"He's a xenobiologist, my dear. Yes that's him!" Karl began waddling up the dusty rise to meet them. "Neville, it's good to see you!" Karl extended one pudgy hand to his friend, who shook it fondly.

"Likewise, my dear fellow, likewise." Karl, completely ignoring Tito, grabbed Neville by the wrist and almost dragged him down the rise to where Belinda stood waiting. Karl was acting like a young boy bringing a new girlfriend home to meet the parents for the first time as he came barreling up to Belinda, dragging the now flustered Neville behind him.

"Dr. Belinda Osborne, I'd like to introduce my learned friend, Professor Neville Whitt!"

Neville eagerly shot out his right hand while he propped his oversized circular steel rim glasses back up onto the bridge of his thin, bony nose.

"Delighted to meet you, simply delighted. Karl has often spoken of you, my dear. You know he holds you in high regard and…"

Tito stepped between them with a somewhat concerned

expression on his face. For a moment, Belinda fancied she heard Neville and Karl conversing in heated tones, "That was frightfully rude," and, "The man simply has no manners whatsoever!" She dismissed the two and gave Tito her full attention.

"I know who tooka the skull, Belinda," he said in a hushed tone. Belinda looked rightfully concerned and at that she and Tito left Karl and Neville debating the lack of good manners. Belinda stopped by one of the large fuel hoppers near the vehicles, and Tito, looking around him nervously, followed her behind the huge rust patched container.

"It was me. I'm the one who tooka the skull Belinda."

Belinda's face showed evident signs of shock.

"But why, Tito?" She stared at him. He was a handsome man despite his age. His dark but slightly graying hair lay in an almost flaxen wave across his forehead, his eyes were dark and mysterious, and his broad jaw was rough with a three-day growth. He was a well-built man and he was in pretty good shape for someone of forty-seven.

"I heard footsteps outside-a my tent last night, so I take-a look to see who it is, but I see no one. I figure soma one mighta be looking for the skull so I hide it and put in the sandstone to fool them!" Belinda's shocked expression subsided slightly.

"Where's the skull now?"

Tito smiled slightly as he gently tapped the side of the massive container. "It's a safe!" he said.

Belinda put her hand to her chest and gave a half chuckle.

"Don't ever do anything like that again, *please!*" Tito relaxed a little and the warm expression she was so fond of returned to his face.

"I sorry, Belinda, but I wasn't sure who to tell last night!" They both laughed a little and emerged from their hiding place.

"I need a coffee!" Tito nodded in agreement and they set off for the canteen.

"Tito, can I ask a favor?"

Tito smiled at her as they walked. "I'd do anything for you, Belinda!"

She grinned and rubbed the back of her neck.

"Would you mind talking to the two laborers from the village? They seemed spooked last night. They saw the skull."

Tito's smile vanished.

"If Lula and Perez saw the skull, they going to wanna leave here because they're very superstitious about the legend."

Belinda stopped dead in her tracks a few feet from the canteen.

"Just a minute Tito, how did you know Karl had the skull with him?"

Tito blushed. "How da you think it got througha security at the airport? I have many friends here."

Belinda shook her head in disbelief. "I see that I'm going to have to keep an eye on you. No more secrets, okay?"

Tito nodded and walked off to tell the rest of the team that they could pack away their possessions and return to work, after which he headed over to the tent occupied by Lula and Perez to allay the fears that the sight of the skull had evidently aroused in them. Belinda sat down with her elbows on the table; she cupped her hands over her face. A few moments later she felt the table creak with that weight of persons sitting down opposite her. She slowly lowered her hands and there opposite her, sat portly Karl and lanky Neville, both with their hands clasped in front of them wearing faces of parental concern. Belinda sighed heavily, got up and went straight for the coffee pot.

After returning with a steaming mug of coffee, Belinda sat down again opposite Karl and Neville.

"My dear Belinda, have you had any luck with 'you know what'?"

She took a sip of coffee, cupped both hands around the mug, looked up at Karl and nodded gently.

"Oooh, where is it? Is it safe?"

She gave a sidelong glance of the direction of Neville. Karl frowned at her and then the penny dropped in his brain.

"Oh, it's quite alright my dear; the obscure reference was for the benefit of unwanted listeners. Neville knows all about it!"

Belinda looked around. Apart from a trio of laborers working in the dirt about a hundred yards away, the canteen was deserted.

"Tito hid it for safe keeping," she told him, which she knew wasn't the best thing to say at a time like this. She saw him instantly puff up like a blowfish and his rubicund features seemed to flush that little bit brighter than normal.

"Well, I suppose *he* does know best!"

Neville sat there with a face of pure indifference, eyes on the examination tent across the way from where they sat. Belinda picked up on this and, leaving Karl to deflate and cool off, she leaned over to Neville.

"I believe we have something that might greatly interest you, Professor Whitt."

Neville perked up and smiled broadly at her. "I thought you'd never ask!" he replied, and with that Neville and Belinda left the table and walked off, leaving Karl sat there, seething.

It wasn't long after Belinda and Neville began unpacking the crate that contained the bizarre skeletal remains, when Karl, realizing that he was complaining to an audience that consisted of a few empty tables and a bubbling coffee pot, came waddling over to them.

"It's absolutely magnificent," Neville exclaimed as they removed the skeleton from the packing straw. The straw was covered with the same blue gunk that Tito and the others had gotten covered in when they moved the skeleton from its grave. Neville examined a clump of the jellified straw.

"That's interesting. It appears that the creature's bone marrow has liquefied!"

Belinda thought this strange because of the age of the bones. "Surely the marrow should have fossilized along with the bones?"

Neville, completely unfazed, looked at Belinda and smiled. His pale, watery eyes seemed greatly magnified by the lenses of his huge silver rimmed spectacles. "Dr. Osborne, these bones aren't fossilized, or at least not completely."

She looked puzzled. "But the skeleton's been in the ground for nearly eight thousand years. How do you explain that?"

It was at this point that Belinda realized that she had just said that fatal word *explain*. Neville seemed to instantly switch to lecture mode and he was off!

"Well you see, the structure of these bones are vastly different from yours or mine because they are so incredibly dense in construction. This in turn points to a high-gravity environment, and the marrow incidentally contains high concentrations of cobalt, hence the blue color of the marrow...."

After about half an hour, Belinda stopped him in mid sentence. "I'm sorry, Professor, but how can you know all this from simply looking at this skeleton?"

Neville seemed, for a moment, dumbstruck, then he turned to where Karl sat, puffing on another fine Havana, then to the skeleton and finally back to Belinda.

"Ha! You mean he didn't tell you?" He turned back to Karl

"You didn't tell her?" Karl suddenly looked up at Neville, slightly surprised.

"He didn't tell you!"

Belinda was beginning to get agitated. "He didn't tell me what?" she said sharply.

Neville's grin broadened. "My dear Belinda, I have worked for several non-government organizations that have been studying extraterrestrial remains and artifacts for a good few years now. This chap will be the third of his kind I've seen, but the first in such excellent condition!"

He quickly put down the straw he had in his hand and went to one of the bags he'd brought with him, leaving Belinda glaring at Karl, who sat there now with the face of a scolded schoolchild.

Neville returned with something in a wooden case.

"Here it is!" he exclaimed. Behind him, Karl gave a sigh of relief as Neville stood blocking him from Belinda's view.

"Here's what?" she said hotly.

"This was found buried with the second skeleton we excavated two years ago. It's remained in my personal possession until Karl told me about you, so I'd like you to, let's say, look after it for me."

He produced a wooden box similar to Karl's and sat it down on the table next to the skeleton. As he was busy unlocking the box, Belinda sidestepped to bring Karl into view. As she thought, he had scurried off outside to let her "concentrate."

"There we are! For you," said Neville as he handed Belinda a rounded object covered with a thick piece of calico. She took it from him and removed the sheet, and in her hands sat a skull, a skull the same dimensions as the emerald skull Karl had shown her, but this one was of deepest ruby red.

A Fatal Accident?

Belinda stared at the skull in her hands. Neville stood there with his hands clasped behind his back, smiling broadly and rocking to and fro on the balls of his feet.

"Nice, isn't it!" he said.

Belinda didn't answer him. She just stared at the skull, and as before, she noticed at its center, this skull too had what appeared to be a tiny silvery sphere.

"You'll have to pardon my skepticism on this point, Professor, but it's not every day a run-of-the-mill archeologist like myself is given the opportunity to study such, well, such unusual artifacts."

She placed the skull on the table, but no sooner had she done this when Perez, one of the site laborers, came wandering into the tent, evidently looking for his partner. He stood in the entrance to the tent looking at Belinda with a vacant half smile on his face. Belinda looked up and saw him and she quickly moved in front of the table so as to obscure the second skull from view.

"Scuzé senorita" he said in a soft voice.

Belinda smiled at him and started to walk towards him when she heard Neville say, "It really is quite fine, isn't it Karl." Belinda froze. Behind her, Neville had picked up the skull and proceeded to walk over to Karl with it.

Perez saw the skull, and his face contorted in horror, his eyes bulged like saucers and he let out a terrified, inarticulate scream before bolting out of the tent and running wildly away down the rise to the excavation site.

"Jesus Christ!" cried Belinda in frustration. She turned to see Neville standing there with a face of blank astonishment.

"Odd fellow," he remarked.

"There's a reason I was hiding the skull from him, Professor!"

She turned from the two men and darted out of the tent after Perez. The last thing she needed now was an excuse from any of the workers to stop working and, heaven forbid, leave the site. She found Perez gesticulating wildly to the other excavators in the group and thought that at any moment there would be a mass exodus of people from the site. It was imperative that this find stay under wraps but instead of the group hysteria she expected, many of them just look at each other and started laughing at poor Perez. At this insulting response, Perez flapped his arms wildly and darted off to the vehicle compound with Belinda hot on his heels.

"Where the hell is Tito when I need him?" she muttered to herself as she jogged after the panic-stricken Perez. She finally reached the vehicle compound, but the place was deserted. She stopped in the center of a line of dusty trucks and cars, scanning the area around her. Hands on hips, she cursed again under her breath. Rapidly thinking where he could have gotten to, she didn't notice the thin, shadowy figure that was moving behind her on the other side of the line of vehicles. Moments later, she was brought to her senses by a muffled scream that came from the far end of the line of trucks.

Spurred into action, she bolted over to the source of the scream, and there by the rear wheels of a pickup was Perez.

He was crumpled in a heap with a huge gash at the back of his head. Crimson blood spilled out from the wound only to be absorbed by the sandy earth.

"Oh, dear god!" she said as she bent down to where his still body lay.

"HELP, SOMEBODY HELP!" she screamed.

Moments later, Lula and three others came over to where she knelt next to Perez's body.

Lula seemed dumbstruck at the sight but then began to weep frantically at the sight of his friend lying in the dust, dead. A minute or so later, Tito came running over.

"What'sa happened?"

He fell silent at the sight.

"Give me hand with him before we draw to much attention. Quickly, help me get him into the canteen." Without speaking, Tito grabbed Perez's limp arms, and together they hastily got him into the canteen tent and covered him over with a tablecloth.

"I can't imagine who coulda dona such a thing?" Belinda was shaking violently. She was used to seeing dead things, but by the time she got to them, several thousand years had passed and the question of murder was never entertained.

"Are you alright, Belinda?" Tito asked. He placed one big hand on her arm and this seemed to bring her around.

"What? Oh yeah. I'll be okay."

"Sure?"

She nodded at him, but he could see heavy tears welling up in her green eyes.

"I go talk to the guys, okay?"

She nodded again as she put her hand to her mouth. Tito left the tent just as Karl and Neville entered.

"Belinda? What's this hullabaloo about?"

She looked up at the two men who were both slightly redder than usual, which was a sure sign they had been running. Belinda composed herself as best she could.

"Perez has been murdered, Karl." It took a few seconds for the word *murdered* to sink in.

"Murdered?" he gasped "By who?" he vacantly asked.

"I don't know!" she snapped.

Karl realized that it was stupid question given the circumstances. He rested his folded parasol against one of the tables and placed an arm across her shoulders; she turned and hugged him as she burst into floods of tears.

Neville at this point decided he could be of assistance elsewhere and left the tent to find Tito.

Half an hour or so later, Tito came back to the tent closely followed by Neville, whose graying hair was now a straggling mess about his shoulders.

By this time, Belinda had been consoled by Karl and was now resolute that they would get to the bottom of this heinous crime come hell or high water.

"What news, my man?" he asked Tito.

"It'sa not good Meester Weston. Half da men have run away. They say it'sa da skulls thata killed Perez." Karl straightened up

"We must get them back. If they talk about what we've found here, we can say goodbye to the whole bloody thing!"

Belinda looked horrified. "Karl! How can you say that? A man is dead because of those bloody skulls!"

Karl realized that he'd put his foot in it again. "I'm sorry, Belinda. This was supposed to be the find of the millennium, our find!"

She shook her head. "I want nothing more to do with any of this if it's going to cost lives. No dig's so important that it overrules human life!"

Neville took Belinda by the arm. "Come on, my dear; let's get you some nice, strong coffee. Karl, it may be prudent to get our departed friend there into one of the preservation bags and then get him to the nearest hospital." Karl looked at Neville then down at the floor, forefinger resting on his lips.

"MORTUARY!" he exclaimed. Neville gave a sarcastic little nod and turned with Belinda out of the tent. With most of the work being done by Tito, the two men got Perez's body into a fresh preservation bag and into the back of Tito's truck.

Within minutes they were driving away from the plateau and down the dusty track that led to what passed for the main road out here. As they wound their way along the dusty dirt track, neither of them saw the little black convoy of vehicles on the horizon heading in the direction of the plateau. A few hours later, they reached the city limits. Karl saw lots of signposts but didn't understand a single one so as navigator on this grizzly errand; he was about as useful to Tito as a chocolate teapot. They finally saw the hospital and pulled up outside. It was incredibly busy inside so Tito ordered Karl to stay in the truck while he tried to get some assistance without drawing too much attention to the fact that a forty-seven-year-old Mexican and an overweight, sweaty Englishman had just pulled up in a truck with a dead Peruvian teenager in a body bag for luggage.

It wasn't long until Karl got bored of waiting and decided to stretch his legs. He opened the door of the truck and slammed it squarely into the vehicle parked next to him, which just happened to be a police patrol car.

Not realizing what he had done, Karl proceeded to leave the vehicle and waddle off to the entrance to the hospital. But before he had taken a couple of paces, he felt a heavy hand come down on his shoulder.

"Uno memento, senor?" said a gruff voice. Karl turned to face a middle-aged man with a wide handlebar moustache in official police garb, staring at him with a distinctly angry expression. Karl being Karl was completely oblivious of his situation; bad enough that he stuck out like a sore thumb in his white linen suit and Panama hat, but to top it all, he had now "criminally damaged" a police vehicle while his own contained a corpse.

The police officer glared at Karl, who simply beamed nervously back at him with a certain childlike innocence

"Good evening, Officer!" he squeaked. "And—how—may—I—be—of—assistance?" he said in a slow and slightly patronizing manner. The police officer simply bared his teeth at the little man and pointed back at his vehicle with the big, wedge-shaped dent in his door. He babbled something very quickly at Karl, who, whilst watching the police officer's hands gesticulating wildly, slowly realized what he had done. At this point, Karl's generous nature became his worst enemy as he withdrew his wallet and proceeded to offer the police officer a cash donation towards the repair of his car. This served only to enrage the officer to the point of exploding, and without further notice, Karl found himself being arrested for attempting to bribe an officer and thrust up against the nearest vehicle.

His hands were shackled before being turned around again and frog-marched towards the officer's waiting car. Just then, Tito emerged from the side door of the hospital's mortuary wing to see Karl being bundled into the back of the police car. He heard Karl pleading with the officer.

"Now see here, my good man! Ouch! Watch what you're doing! I just...oof!"

Tito sprinted up to the car and tried to reason with the officer who was desperately trying to close the car door with Karl squirming inside. When he saw Tito shouting at the officer, he beamed at him, thinking that this little misunderstanding would soon be resolved, but, to his horror, the officer arguing with Tito headed for their truck. Karl's heart seemed to skip a beat, but in a flash, Tito was after him, and before Karl knew what was going on, Tito, in a fit of desperation to prevent the officer from seeing their grim cargo, had pulled the nightstick out of the officer's holster and clonked him squarely on the head. The officer grunted and slumped into a heap between the two vehicles. Tito, panting heavily, glared at Karl through the car window.

"Mr. Weston, get your fat arse outta here and help me!" Karl, in blank astonishment, almost mechanically scrambled out of the car and scurried around to where Tito had already started to remove the boy's body from the back of the truck.

"Meester Weston, you getta that one." He nodded in the direction of the unconscious officer. Karl, not being used to such brutish behavior, took several glances between Tito and the officer.

"Pick 'im up, he's not dead. Just unconscious." Cautiously so as not to be observed, Tito darted across the car park and into the darkened side door he had came out of to deposit the body of poor Perez on a gurney. A moment later he reappeared and gasped at what he saw. Karl, still with hands shackled and evidently not being terribly strong, was rolling the unconscious body of the officer across the car park in plain view of the main entrance. The powers that be deemed it fit this evening for Karl Weston to get away with a great many things, and not being caught rolling the unconscious body of a police officer across a hospital car park was just one of them because as Karl emerged from behind a row of vehicles, an ambulance with sirens blaring roared into the car park and clipped the corner of the police car so that the rear door that Karl escaped from earlier popped open.

With one good shove, the police officer's body conveniently rolled into position a few feet from the vehicle, and as the paramedics, thinking they'd caused an accident, descended from the ambulance to aid the stunned police officer, a fat little man walked smartly from between two cars and displayed a face of pure theatrical surprise at the sight of the felled officer and the busy paramedics bustling around him.

Without anyone noticing, the little fat man met up with a tall broad man, and together they inconspicuously clambered into their truck and drove away into the night.

"I feel absolutely terrible," whimpered Karl as they drove back up the lonely dirt trail to the encampment upon the desolate plateau.

"At least he'll be-a treated with soma respect there. Imagine what would've happened if we left his body uppa here!"

"Fair point," said Karl glumly, after which, the rest of the journey was accomplished in complete silence.

As the truck approached the encampment, Karl craned his head forward as if to look beyond the dusty, dirt-smeared windscreen

"It looks like they've got a bonfire going up there!" Tito also looked hard through the dirty glass

"I don't think that's any bonfire!" he exclaimed as he floored the accelerator and catapulted Karl back into his seat, causing him to squeak like a dog's chew toy.

With a screech of tires and a cloud of dust, they came to an abrupt stop about thirty feet from the main tent, which by now was nothing more than a blazing frame of buckling aluminum. Karl also noticed that one of the two Dirt Cat all-terrain vehicles were missing; the other, along with the remaining trucks and motorcycles, was in blazing ruins.

Their camp had been completely destroyed by fire. The thing that was most worrisome was that there was not a soul to bee seen. Karl stood there in blank astonishment until Tito brought him to his senses with a heavy hand on his shoulder.

"Look at this, Meester Weston." Karl spun around to Tito pointing at the ground, indicating a massive number of fresh, additional vehicle tracks.

"Bandits," Tito said with a snarl.

"No, I don't think so!" said Karl in a rather inquisitive tone.

He bent down and looked closely at the tracks.

"These tracks have been made by something large and heavy, like an armored car—several actually, and I sincerely doubt that bandits have those!"

Tito looked quite taken aback. "How you know this?"

Karl looked up at Tito and gave a sullen little smirk. "Because, dear fellow, I love military vehicles. It's something of a hobby of mine, among other things, and I've been for enough rides and seen enough of these vehicles to know what kind of tracks they leave!" Tito was surprised to say the least; this little fat yuppie had his uses after all! Between them, they circumnavigated the entire camp and found only a few clues as to what might have happened.

Evidently there had been a rush, a surprise attack and there had been scuffles, but ultimately it appeared that whoever the assailants were, they had won.

Tito walked back over to the truck with Karl quickly scurrying behind. It wasn't until Tito was seated in the truck that he noticed

Karl wander off to the left. He watched for a moment or so and then got back out of the truck and followed him. Karl was standing about forty feet from the truck, just beyond the light from the fire. His shoulders were hunched and he seemed to be weeping.

"What'sa wrong, Meester Weston?" Tito's sentence was cut short by the sight of what Karl was standing over.

Lying face up with a bullet wound in his left shoulder was Neville Witt. Karl was shaking.

"My best friend," he kept saying over and over. Tito took Karl by the arm and turned him away from the body.

"We *will* finda out who did this, Meester Weston, I promise you that."

Karl was blubbering and sniffing as he spoke. "But he is—was my best friend! I'd known him for thirty-two years!"

There was a groan behind them and then reedy voice of Neville Whitt was heard, contradicting Karl.

"It's thirty-three actually."

Both Tito and Karl Spun around to see Neville sitting up, nursing what was actually a light flesh wound. Karl's face lit up and then turned sour as he lunged at Neville, who was looking quite startled by this.

Tito grabbed Karl by the scruff of his collar and yanked him back like a dog on a leash.

"I thought you were dead!" Neville looked at his war wound.

"I also did for a while. I thought it would be best to play dead rather than get captured."

After all had calmed down, Tito helped Neville into the truck and they set off again, in the direction of the foreign tracks, Neville giving a vibrant commentary along the way.

Chapter 5

Disappearance and Destruction

"It all began a little after you left to take that poor boy's body away," began Neville.

"We were sitting down in the mess tent, and Dr. Osborne and I were talking about the skeleton you had unearthed, when all of a sudden, as if from nowhere, nine big, black truck-things came roaring into the camp. Before I knew what was happening, about thirty rather rude and burly men had jumped from the vehicles and started encircling us. They had guns, you know. Big ones too!"

Karl wore a grave expression as he listened to Neville's account.

"Go on," he insisted.

"Hmm, oh yes, sorry. So there we were, sitting in absolute disbelief with thirty guns trained on us. Then I heard that voice. I will never forget it. Through the gunmen, came the man who had us at his mercy. He came up to our table, sat down and laughed at us in that awful guffawing Texas accent of his!"

Karl's eyes nearly popped out of his head.

"A Texan? Hey, did he have a scar on his right cheek, Neville?"

Neville seemed to be vacant again.

"Hmm, a scar, um…now come to mention it, I think he did. And there was the other man who joined him shortly after who looked like a weasel. You know, thin and shifty looking with close-set eyes. I tried to reason with them, and that's when that thin fellow shot at me, no manners whatsoever!"

Karl slammed his fist down hard on the dashboard

"HOW DARE HE, HOW BLOODY DARE HE!" Karl shouted.

Tito looked from Karl to Neville and back to Karl

"Who is *he*, Meester Weston?" he asked. Karl's eyes burned with rage, the angriest Tito had ever seen him.

"Marcus bloody Deveraux," he seethed.

"Who?" asked Tito, Karl tried to clam down a little. He took a deep breath and began.

"Marcus Deveraux is an ex-partner of mine from when I dabbled in the rare antiquities market and a ruthless beggar to say the least. He and his new business associate, Wilhelm Reichstein, a German arms dealer, have destroyed countless lives in their search for the riches of avarice! I thought I'd seen the last of him when I heard he was standing trial in Algiers for arms and relic smuggling. He obviously got away and somehow found out about the skulls and tracked us down. DAMN HIM TO HELL!" Karl exclaimed.

It was at this point that Neville interrupted.

"I don't want to bother anyone, but I am bleeding a bit." Tito stopped the truck with a jerk, making Karl squeak again as he shot forward, nearly head butting the windscreen. Tito unbuckled his seatbelt and turned to face Neville.

"Let's have a look," he said. Neville pulled his shirt back to reveal an inch-long crimson gash across his left shoulder that was still trickling with blood.

"You'll live," he exclaimed. "It's a just a bullet graze." He handed Neville a handkerchief from his pocket.

"Hold this on to it to stoppa the bleeding."

"You don't have any water do you?" asked Neville. Tito reached over to the glove box and pulled out a bottle of Tequila. "Thisa will make you feela a bit better," he said. Neville scrutinized the bottle for a few moments and then pulled out the cork, took a gulp and wheezed like he'd just been punched in the stomach. "Thank you very—*cough*—much!" he replied in a croaky voice. They started off again into the night, following the tracks of the Deveraux convoy.

After what seemed and interminable time, the tracks stopped. Tito didn't realize at first, so he had to reverse several meters to see where they ended.

Karl had been dozing and Neville was insensible due to the copious amount of tequila he'd consumed. Karl came to and sat up when he realized they had stopped.

"Is something the matter, Tito?"

Tito rummaged about in the door compartment for a minute or so and then produced a battered old torch.

"The tracks have stopped, Meester Weston." Karl looked alarmed. Without another word, they both got out of the vehicle and looked around them for some signs of where they might pick up the scent again. They couldn't.

To the left of them, the land sloped up an embankment some forty to fifty feet quite steeply, and to the right, a sharp incline down into a rift several hundred feet below.

"Well, they didn't go up, and they didn't go down," said Karl, completely perplexed.

Several hours later in the half light of early dawn, Karl and Tito sat at the base of the embankment. Tito was smoking a cigarette and Karl was fiddling with his now sooty and dirt-splashed coat. They both looked around at the truck when they heard the insensible Neville fidgeting and moaning. A minute later he had stumbled out of the truck and rubbed his face with his hands. His hair was all over the place, his glasses were cocked at an obscure angle on his beak-like nose and he had the distinct look of an old bloodhound about him.

"Are you all right, Meester Whitt?" asked Tito, trying to suppress chuckle.

"Wha...? Yes...fine...I think....Why have we stopped?"

Karl explained about the tracks and the dead end with no clues to go on and no idea of the whereabouts of Belinda and the others. With almost mechanical reaction, Neville snapped out of his stupor, brushed his hair back and straightened his spectacles. "Well, I thought it would be perfectly clear what happened to them don't you?" he said in a clear, reedy textbook tone.

Tito looked bemused to say the least.

"What?" Karl said with growing excitement.

"Up," said Neville. "They went up."

"What, helicopter?" asked Tito.

"No, look at the dirt. There's no downdraft disturbance of the earth." They looked at the ground. Indeed it seemed that Neville was right. The tracks just stopped.

"I think I know where they are," said Neville slowly. Tito jumped to his feet. Neville now had the full and undivided attention of this unlikely duo.

"Well?" blurted Karl.

"Tito, are you familiar with the ruins of the butterfly plaza?" asked Neville. Tito nodded slowly.

"Do you know where the ruins are situated?" Tito smiled at Neville, patted him on the left shoulder and headed for the truck.

"I got a rough idea, Mr. Whitt."

"Are you all right, old boy? You've gone a tad pale." asked Karl. Neville cradled his left shoulder and whimpered.

"Oh. Still a bit sore, eh?"

Within minutes they were racing down the side of the plateau. Karl was hanging on to the door handle for dear life, and Neville, who intelligent as he was, was fighting frantically to buckle his seat belt whilst being buffeted about in the back.

"Exactly what is this 'butter flying thingy' thing anyway?" asked Karl in a shaky voice.

"Karl, you really must research these little projects of yours properly first!" said Neville.

"The butterfly plaza is the fabled site of the temple of Venus, The original worshipping place for the thirteen crystal skulls of Lubaantun. It was thought to be the most grand of all the temples of the ancient world. Some even say that its powers rivaled that of Atlantis, if it ever existed. Its remains are thought to lie at the top of the Andes, near the Cordillera Occidental. Some believe that it was destroyed when the inhabitants released a new power source so great that they couldn't control it and it destroyed the temple and the city along with it!" Tito gave a little skeptical laugh as Karl craned his neck around to look at Neville.

"So, Neville, how far is it then?" Neville produced a little black atlas from his pocket

"Look, we're here, just outside Trujillo and the ruins are reported to be here. Not far from Huaraz. It's about one hundred miles, give or take a few."

"It's a fair distance then!" said Karl, still bobbing up and down as he spoke.

"Yes, but we should be there by nightfall assuming me maintain our current locomotive velocity."

At that point, fate deemed it fit to play the trio another poor hand. The engine gurgled, spluttered, skipped twice and died.

The truck rolled to a dead stop and Tito slammed his hands down on the wheel and cursed in Mexican so the others couldn't understand him. Karl knew, regardless of the language, a curse when he heard it.

"Oh dear, what now?" asked Neville.

Tito got out and walked around to the front of the truck to pop the hood. Karl and Neville scrambled out too. "Um, can we be of some assistance?" asked Karl. Tito looked at the pair. What a double act they made. He gave a sarcastic little laugh and shook his head.

"I think that's a no, Neville," said Karl dryly. The two gentlemen then decided to head up the nearest small hillock to get their bearings.

"What are those, Neville?" asked Karl squinting into the distance.

"What? Oh, I think they're llamas." They both stood with their backs to Tito, hands above their eyes like sun visors.

Tito was too busy cursing, swearing and banging engine components to see the two men wander off in the direction of the little herd of llamas. About half an hour later, Tito realized just how quiet it was and that he hadn't been bothered by either Karl or Neville.

He turned around to look for the two men and was greeted by the foaming, stinking mouths of a three llamas. He recoiled in surprise, shocking one of the animals into spitting at him. He stood up, resting himself against the truck as he wiped the saliva from his shirt.

"Splendid idea!" said a voice, and for a split second Tito thought he was hallucinating. Had that llama just spoken?

Then he realized that it hadn't because from behind the llama closest to him, the rosy, sweating faces of Karl Weston and Neville Whitt appeared.

"Hello! We're back and look what we found!"

Tito didn't know what to say.

"I'MA NOT RIDING A LLAMA!" he exclaimed. The two men looked at each other and started chortling.

"What'sa so funny?" asked Tito.

"Haven't you ever seen a wild west film?" asked Neville.

An hour or so later, the three llamas, which had been shackled to the front of the truck with some old tow-ropes were now pulling it along as they happily chased a large bunch of juicy cactus roots that was being dangled from a makeshift fishing pole in front of them by Neville, who sat strapped onto the bonnet while Tito steered.

Karl leaned out of his window, hat in hand.

"YAHOO! I've always wanted to do that! Friendly sort of creatures aren't they!" he said in that excited squeaky voice of his.

Tito just sighed.

Chapter 6
The Winged Serpent

They actually covered a great deal of distance that day despite traveling under llama power, and they arrived at the town of Chimbote around seven that evening where they were able to repair the truck and get water, supplies, a hot meal and a wash.

Of course this all came at the expense of "Meester Weston," whom the shopkeepers loved very dearly.

"I had better get a damn good meal for this," Karl said hotly, shoving his wallet back into the inside pocket of his jacket as they sat in the little bar drinking odd-tasting liquor.

A few minutes later the barman came wandering over and placed in front of them three bowls of what looked like some sort of gray, lumpy stew.

Without a word, Tito attacked the food ravenously. Neville took a little more tactile approach and tasted a bit on the tip of his tongue, and Karl just stared at his.

"Actually it is really rather good!" exclaimed Neville. "Try it!

You always liked broadening your palette, have a little taste. It's not unlike the beef stew at the rotary club in Westminster."

Karl risked a nibble, savored the taste then proceeded to devour it spoonful by spoonful.

"This is actually really good!" said Karl.

"I wonder what it is?" he turned around in his chair and caught the barman's eye, and in good old British tradition, he signified his satisfaction by pointing at the bowl and rubbing his stomach. Then he pointed to his head and shook it. The barman seemed to understand, laughed and pointed to the wall behind him. Karl looked in the direction the barman had pointed and his face dropped. At the same time Neville dropped his spoon and suddenly found it hard to swallow.

Hanging on the wall behind them was a large old picture of a most majestic looking...llama.

Karl suddenly lost his appetite, Neville too it would seem, but to Tito, food was food no matter where it came from, and not wanting to insult the barkeep or let good food go to waste, Tito devoured the remains of Neville's and Karl's stew as well.

The silence was suddenly broken by Tito, who slammed both palms down on the table and pushed himself away in his chair

"We got a get going!"

Neville and Karl both shook off their sickened looks and turned their attention to Tito.

"Right, let's get going!" said Karl with an air of military determination. Tito waved his hand in thanks at the barkeep, and Karl, not wanting to appear ungrateful for their most unusual and disturbing meal, politely tipped his hat the to the barman as they left. Neville was already out the door and darting for the truck. Karl seemed somewhat more relaxed once they were on their way again. Neville on the other hand was a little preoccupied in his mind with the fate of the three llamas they had left back in Chimbote. It had seemed a surreal evening, stopping for a meal knowing full well that Belinda may well be in danger, and Karl aired his thoughts on this but Tito reminded him that they needed to have their wits about them and being starving may well have proved a serious distraction.

By early morning of the next day, they had almost arrived at the foot of the mountains upon which sat the fabled site of the temple of Venus. As they approached the foothills, they clearly saw the tell tale signs of recent intense activity.

Tito stopped the truck just by a large boulder that marked the start of the incline up into the foothills. All three got out from the truck and stared at the ground in front of them, unable to believe what they saw. No more than twenty feet from them was a shallow depression in the ground about two feet deep and at least fifty feet wide. What was so odd was that it was a perfect circle, as if something very large and very heavy had landed there, and very recently.

To confuse them even more, heading out from the depression in the direction of the foothills were tire tracks of a great many vehicles. Karl looked behind him in the direction they had just come and he saw that there was only a single set of tracks, their tracks. Neville gave a little laugh.

"See! I said they went up."

"What to do now?" Karl said to himself as he fanned his wet brow with his hat in the rising heat of the morning.

Neville was the first to answer, making Tito smile a little.

"Is anyone up for a spot of mountaineering?" Tito returned to the truck and pulled out a beaten old rucksack and began piling in equipment that Karl had paid for from Chimbote.

"Did we remember the water this time?" asked Neville. Tito lifted up the tequila bottle making Neville's face drop.

"It's okay, Meester Whitt, it's water!" he said with a chuckle.

Within an hour, they had traversed the lowest of the foothills and Tito realized that they weren't as steep as he first reckoned.

"Wait here for me, I go get the truck. Okay!"

With an obviously gratified sigh, Karl flopped down on the ground and took a sip from the water-filled Tequila bottle.

"Fancy a drop, Neville?" asked Karl with a pant.

Neville took the bottle and took a long drink, turning as he did so. He nearly spat the contents over Karl as he coughed and spluttered, fighting to stop choking.

"What the devil's wrong with you? Are you alright?"

Neville handed the bottle back to Karl who sniffed the contents cautiously. Neville, who was still coughing, pointed to an area behind Karl, who shuffled around to see what Neville was pointing at.

The bottle fell from Karl's hand, rolled away a few feet and decanted its contents into the sandy earth. Karl struggled to his feet and as before raised a hand to act as a sun visor. Both He and Neville stood motionless, staring out across the plain below them. Far off in the distance, just above the horizon was a large, black wedge shape. It was slowly gliding through the air towards the mountain top, flanked, they noticed, by two helicopters. Neither of them spoke as they watched the unearthly shape drift ever closer to a point far above them on the mountain. They must have been standing there for some time because the next thing they recalled was the sound of a revving engine as Tito approached. The pair seemed totally oblivious to Tito's return because they still stood there after the object and its escorts had vanished into the side of the mountain high above them, possibly hoping to catch another glimpse of this peculiar craft. Tito came up behind them, looked at them, looked up at the mountain and looked back at them again.

"Whatsa up, chaps?" he said in a very dodgy English imitation. Karl squeaked and Neville jumped at the sound of Tito's voice.

"Really, Tito, must you sneak up on us like that?" Karl spat.

Tito looked at Karl, then at the truck and decided not to say anything. After Karl and Neville had digested what they had seen, they told Tito. He listened intently to the two gentlemen as they imparted their story to him. He looked both confused and concerned at what he had heard.

"Right, ina thè truck, Now!" he snapped. And once again, Neville and Karl were being buffeted about as the drove from the foot hills up the mountain as far as they could. About halfway up the west face, they stopped for a break. The sun was already halfway through its western decent and the sky was beginning to show tinges of burnt orange. It was Neville that first heard it, a low *budda, budda, budda*

51

sound. He then recognized it as the spinning of helicopters rotor blades.

"HIDE!" cried Tito and they all scrabbled for meager cover on the barren mountainside. Karl found shelter behind and old rock formation and not a moment too soon. The helicopter slowly whirled by as he ducked down. It was at this point that he caught a glimpse of the emblem on the side. It was a winged serpent with the letters M and D below it. "It has to be Deveraux!" Karl cursed to himself as the helicopter passed.

In their haste to hide, they had left the truck out in the open, so whoever was piloting the helicopter must have seen it. This in turn eliminated their chances of the element of surprise.

They had no choice but to wait for the helicopter to pass and then dart back down the slope to the truck. "What will we do now?" Karl gesticulated.

"I don't know what the dickens is going on here, but I think we're in way over our heads," said Neville sharply.

"I'm not giving up yet," snapped Tito. "Belinda may still be up there and we gotta go get her."

Both Karl and Neville were looking at Tito in abject horror.

"Are you serious? This is getting ridiculous; we're scientists, not the bloody A-team! Maybe we can be amicable with them," cried Neville.

Tito was getting angry. "They shot you, Mr. Whitt! Nothing amicable about that!" he shouted.

Neville frowned and looked back at the helicopter, he knew Tito was right. The helicopter made another pass and slowed to a stop and hovered for a few seconds, and then fired a single rocket that blew Tito's truck to smithereens. All three of them recoiled at the explosion, and Karl ended up on his bottom. Suddenly, as if out of nowhere, twenty or more soldiers encircled them. The trio froze when they realized that there were now twenty gun barrels trained on them. As much as he hated to do it, Tito knew that with Neville and Karl in tow, surrender was the only safe option. Karl and Neville both stood there, petrified, staring until the silence was broken by that awful bellowing Texan laugh.

"Well, well, well, if it isn't ma ol' buddy Karl Hubert Weston. Long time no see, Limey!" Karl slowly turned on the spot and stared into a swollen, pockmarked face that was masked by a pair of overly polished aviator-style sunglasses. The fat, porcine features were scored by a nasty looking scar on the right cheek, and the thick, chapped lips and yellowing teeth clenched a ridiculously oversized Havana cigar between them.

"I might have guessed, Marcus bloody Deveraux!" Karl fumed. "Which slime covered rock did you crawl out form under this time?"

Tito and Neville could see that Karl was near to boiling point, but they hoped he would keep his cool, in light of their situation.

"Well now, ain't that just a dan-deee way to greet an ol' friend." Deveraux Chortled as he puffed on his cigar. "Ain't it about time you started singin' that song for me?" Karl seemed for a moment, dumbstruck.

"You know, 'YOU WIN AGAIN!'" said the repugnant Deveraux as he laughed.

"You WILL NOT get away with this Marcus!" barked Karl. "I will not have my friends treated in this manner! DO YOU HEAR ME?"

Neville fancied he actually saw steam rising from Karl's shirt collar Deveraux removed the aviator glasses to reveal the further contamination of his porcine features as he squinted at Karl and the others with his tiny, pig-like eyes. With one fat finger he pointed to the emblem on his jacket.

"See this!" he began "This is authority! I got a helpin' hand from one of my foreign government friends, you know what this is; this here is qua...quer...ques..."

One of the guards stepped forward and whispered something into Deveraux's ear.

"QUETZALCOATL, the winged serpent and it's fully endorsed by the Peruvian government!"

Karl's face took on a very thin smile.

"Still struggling with concept of intelligent grammar, I see! Come to think of it, a snake represents you very well, and what's more, that's total bunkum!" Karl retorted. "No government in their right mind would touch a scoundrel like you with a barge pole!"

Deveraux, in frustration snapped his glasses in his hand with a crack.

"Get these people inside…NOW!" he bellowed.

"Looks like you struck a nerve there, Karl," Neville said, looking incredibly worried.

The three men were buffeted and pushed along the ridge to a concealed steep incline and forced up it. Upon reaching the top, Deveraux pulled a little black control from his pocket, pointed it at the rock face and pushed a button.

They saw a false section the rock face slide back, revealing a large set of heavy metal doors.

One of the guards went up to a keypad by the doors and punched a series of buttons.

There was quiet hiss and the huge doors slid open. Being given hardly any time to take in their new surroundings, the three were pushed and goaded in through the doors and down a long, floodlit corridor in complete silence.

At this point, fear seemed to be rampant among them, and for good reason.

Chapter 7

Friends Reunited

After a lengthy trek down the corridor, the trio were ushered and ultimately pushed into a small room with a single flush-fitting light in the ceiling. The door was slammed hard and locked behind them and they could hear Marcus Deveraux guffawing in that awful tone as he disappeared along the corridor.

"Well, what do we do now?" said Karl.

"We get outta here is what," said Tito and with that he charged at the door and banged on it repeatedly with his fist.

"That's going to achieve a lot," muttered Karl. Tito stepped back, panting and cursing, but at that moment, there was a soft 'click' and the door swung open. Standing in the doorway, flanked by two armed guards, was a tall thin reedy looking man with rodent-like features and jet black hair. "Why all the noise, gentlemen? You are here as guests of Mr. Deveraux and myself."

The tall man stepped over the threshold and looked each of the three up and down.

"Who the hell are you?" asked Tito. The man gave a thin, wry smile.

"I am Wilhelm Reichstein, Mr. Deveraux's…shall we say…business associate." Karl detected a strong German accent, and he didn't like it one bit.

As Reichstein moved around them in the cell, Karl felt his eyes burning into each one of them, trying to determine what made them tick. He returned to the threshold and stood there, hands clasped behind his back, staring at them again.

"Mr. Weston, Professor Whitt, you will both accompany me. The Mexican stays here."

Tito saw red and lunged at Wilhelm. He was perhaps a few inches from grasping the thin man around his scrawny neck when one of the guards stepped in between them and slammed the butt of his rifle into the side of Tito's head. With a muffled grunt, Tito fell to the floor, unconscious. Wilhelm looked completely unfazed by the brutal act

"Come, gentlemen. We mustn't dawdle."

Karl and Neville, both a little shocked, did as they were bid.

They were led down the rest of the corridor to yet another set of thick heavy doors. Again a guard punched in a series of numbers and the big doors slid open.

Inside, the room was massive. A high flat ceiling and bright lighting gave this room the appearance of an operating theater. Sitting at a huge table in the center was Marcus Deveraux, and to his left, with a bruise on her temple and her head on her chest was Belinda.

She sat there with her hands bound together with handcuffs and her chair was also chained to the table with handcuffs.

"You MONSTER!" cried Karl

"Oh, come now, Karl, it's all for effect; she's as free as a bird really," said Deveraux, and with that, he gave a nod and one of the guards approached her and unlocked the shackles.

"I was merely pointing out that I can do what I damn well please here and no one, NO ONE is gonna dictate to me!"

Belinda looked up; her eyes were swollen and it was clear that she had been sedated, quite heavily too. Karl rushed over to her, leaving Neville standing there with the two burly guards on either side of him. He looked very small and fragile between the two gladiatorial clad guards.

"Oh, Belinda, are you alright?" asked Karl as he knelt down beside her in the chair. Belinda looked at him through her red, bloodshot eyes. She uttered the word *skulls* before she became insensible again. Karl looked up at Deveraux who was now accompanied by the rat-like Reichstein

"Skulls," said Reichstein.

"Ha, ha, look what I got, Karl!" said Deveraux as he moved to his left and pulled the small remote control from his pocket.

He pointed it at the wall behind him and a large flat panel slid to one side revealing a recess containing the two skulls found by Belinda and Neville, but these two skulls were in a collection with six others, three on each side. Each one was of a different crystalline hue and Karl saw that as before, the center of each skull housed a tiny silver sphere, all but one. The skull on the extreme right was of a milky blue substance, not unlike marble, but it still had that eerie living presence of all the other skulls.

Karl stood up, jaw open and gaping in awe. Neville was mimicking Karl's expression. Karl slowly walked toward the case. As he did so, several of the guards jumped to attention and started moving toward Karl. With a wave of his hand, Deveraux dismissed them and they fell back.

Neville too followed suit and approached the case. They both reached it together and seemed to be in complete ignorance of each other's presence as they stared at the eight skulls that sat in their glass tomb.

"My god, they're beautiful!" exclaimed Neville to himself.

"May I ask how many people suffered at your hand for you to acquire these?" asked Karl snidely.

"Oh, Karl, now you've gone and hurt ma feelings," chuckled Deveraux, and with a click of his remote, the panel slid back into place obscuring the skulls one more.

"As you can see, gentlemen, I have the upper hand here—again," spat Deveraux.

Reichstein gave a little snigger beside the hulking form of the fat, gloating Texan.

"What hand would that be then, Marcus?" answered Karl dryly. "You are still five skulls short of the full deck, aren't you" He gave a little smirk as he said this.

"Oh, and I suppose you know the whereabouts of the other five do ya?" barked Deveraux.

"Maybe I do." Neville gave Karl a nervous sideways glance.

"Karl!" he said through gritted teeth. "What are you doing?"

Deveraux approached Karl and stopped within centimeters of his face. "Don't try and play games with me, Weston." Karl tried to back away as the stinking tobacco breath and spittle sprayed him.

"If you know where the other five skulls are, you tell me and no harm will come to you or your friends." Karl, despite the foul breath grinned broadly at him.

"Why, Marcus, if I didn't know better, I'd swear that you were threatening me!"

Marcus recoiled a little. He actually looked a little confused. "That's exactly what I'm doing, you stupid little limey shit!"

Karl grinned broadly "Really, bloody feeble effort if you ask me!" Neville nudged Karl in the arm and Karl saw what he was trying to indicate. There was a tiny vein that had popped up on the side of Deveraux's head and he seemed to have developed a nervous twitch in one eye.

"Reichstein!" he bellowed. "Get Laurel and bloody Hardy here outta my sight! That damn girl too!"

Wilhelm Reichstein was already directing the guards as Deveraux stormed off to another set of doors at the other end of the huge room. Within ten minutes, all three of them—Karl, Neville and the still insensible Belinda, were back in the little room along with Tito, who was nursing a badly bruised and cut head.

"What on earth were you doing back there, Karl?" demanded Neville.

"It's quite simple really. When we used to work together, I knew the quickest way to antagonize Marcus Deveraux was to speak to him in the most sarcastic tone possible. He hates it and it makes him feel quite inadequate and angry. So angry in fact that he loses his focus and can't think straight. I knew that would get us out of there."

Neville still looked worried. "Please tell me if you intend to do that again, Karl," he said sheepishly. *At least he hasn't done what he should have done—split us up!* thought Karl with a smile.

Chapter 8
The Not-So-Great Escape

After what seemed like an eternity, Belinda regained full consciousness and sat up, rubbing her head. "Belinda, my dear, are you all right?"

She looked up through bleary eyes at Karl who was standing over her with an expression of motherly concern.

"Where are we?" she asked as she stood up in the confined space.

She looked around to take stock of her new surroundings. Over in the far corner farthest from the door sat Tito with a nasty crimson gash and severe bruising along the right hand side of his face. Next to him, looking like a frightened rabbit, was Neville, pale as usual.

Then she turned back to Karl, still dressed in a now somewhat dusty and mud-splashed white linen suite and a crumpled Panama hat.

"We're the, *ahem*, 'guests' of Mr. Marcus Deveraux. These are our guest quarters. Spartan, but then again Deveraux never did have very good taste and besides—"

Belinda grabbed Karl by the arm, cutting him off in mid sentence. Her eyes wide and staring.

"He's got the skulls and the skeleton!" she exclaimed.

"I know, we've seen them." He nodded in Neville's direction.

"What does he want with us, Karl? I mean what is this place, why are we here?"

Karl opened his mouth but it wasn't his voice that she heard.

"Ah think Ah can answer that one, Miss Osborne." Belinda spun around, and there in the doorway stood the porcine hulk of Marcus Deveraux, flanked by two more of his armed guards. And behind him, the rodent like face of Wilhelm Reichstein was visible, sneering.

"Ah suppose y'all wanna know what I'm up to, don't ya? Well, if you're all good boys and girls, I'll show ya."

He grinned through those fat, blistered lips of his, and Belinda saw the yellow, tobacco-stained teeth that still clenched the remnants of a long dead cigar.

"Take the Mexican and get him patched up. Ah want ma tour group ready in thirty minutes, clear?" The guard on his left gave a nod and marched up to Tito, grabbed him by the arm and more or less dragged him, stumbling out of the cell and down the corridor.

"The rest of you can follow Mr. Reichstein here and get cleaned up." He turned to the little rat-like man and said, "Make sure they get some food as well. Don't want them starvin' on me, now do I!"

He gave a little grunt-like chuckle and a cough before walking off, leaving the remaining guard and Wilhelm Reichstein to lead them down the corridor a few meters to another room where they found washing facilities.

Before closing the door on them, Reichstein grinned evilly at them.

Despite being held captive, Belinda couldn't resist the prospect of a good wash. It might even make her mind less foggy after the sedatives she'd received.

She began to strip off. Karl gave a cry of surprise and Neville walked away, shielding his face with one hand.

"What?" asked Belinda as she had her vest pulled halfway over her head.

"Oh nothing, we'll just be over here looking the other way," said Karl sheepishly.

After they had washed themselves, the lock clicked, the door opened and in walked a guard carrying three bags of what appeared to be beef jerky and three bottles of water.

"Eat" was the only word said by the guard.

"What, no napkins or wine menu?" said Karl sarcastically. The guard glared at him before stomping out and locking the door behind him.

"Hardly the Ritz, is it!" he said with a chuckle as he struggled to open his bag of jerky. "God, I hate this bloody 'poly-whatchamacallit' plastic."

He savagely attacked it with his teeth but to no avail. Suddenly Neville snatched the bag from him and slit the top open with a small penknife.

"There you go old chap!" he said as he handed Karl's bag back to him with a smile. Neville popped a piece of jerky into his mouth and chewed it slowly because he became aware that both Belinda and Karl were staring at him. "Is something wrong?" he asked.

"Where the hell did you get that from?" asked Belinda.

"What, this? I always keep a penknife with me because you never know when you might need it!" he said holding up the knife

"Neville, I think you just found our ticket out of here!" exclaimed Belinda. She gently took the knife off of him and slipped it in the side of her boot. "Don't mind if I borrow this do you? " Neville nodded as he chewed.

"Right, here's what we're going to do."

A few minutes later, the door opened once more and one guard and Reichstein entered.

"On your feet!" spat Reichstein. The trio stood up, and the guard handed his rifle to Reichstein and approached them with three sets of shackles.

"Ladies first, I think," said Reichstein as the guard stood behind

Belinda. In a flash, she shot for the knife and spun around with the blade poised at the guard's jugular vein.

"Drop the gun, Reichstein!" she demanded. Reichstein didn't flinch.

"Well, well. We are sprightly aren't we!" he said in that monotone, droning voice of his. With one swift movement, he raised the gun and fired a single round. Belinda froze; Neville and Karl both jumped with fright. Slowly, the pressure behind the knife decreased as the guard collapsed in a heap on the floor.

"A valiant attempt, dear lady, but as you can see, the troglodytes that my associate hired are expendable. Now, give me the knife, if you please!"

Belinda couldn't believe the sheer disregard for human life in this evil little man. She dropped the knife and kicked it towards Reichstein. He slowly bent down and picked it up, never once taking his eyes off her. As he stood up again he grinned maniacally at them. Belinda grinned back at him, which Reichstein thought was a bit odd, but then he saw Karl grinning as well. Last he looked at Neville, who was smiling and pointing to an area behind Reichstein out in the corridor.

"Come now, even educated people like you honestly don't think that anyone would fall for that old trick, do you?"

Reichstein then felt a tap on his shoulder. He turned around just in time to see a fist heading straight at his face. With a crack, the punch sent him reeling back into the room, landing against one of the benches next to Belinda. He shook his head to try and regain his balance, but Belinda already had the gun and had it pointed at his head. Crimson blood trickled from his nose and lip. He coughed and grinned. "You won't kill me Miss Osborne, you don't have the nerve!" he said as he spat out a mouthful of saliva and blood out at her feet.

"You're right," she said as she lowered the gun barrel. He laughed again but his laugh turned to a grunt of pain as he realized that Belinda had stabbed the muzzle of the gun into his groin.

Neville flinched and Karl bit his bottom lip as he cupped his hands over his groin in a sympathetic gesture. The man who had surprised Reichstein now approached. Tito looked better for a wash and a patch over his facial wound.

"You!" snarled Reichstein. He saw past Tito to the second guard, lying unconscious in the corridor—Tito had evidently overpowered him.

Reichstein was about to speak again, but Tito struck home with another punch that sent the vile little man down to the ground and into the realms of unconsciousness.

They realized their situation almost immediately; only one gun and four of them. They'd have to act quickly if they were to escape. Tito took the rifle and slowly they crept out into the corridor as Neville bent down to retrieve his knife.

Karl closed the door behind him and Neville made a point of removing the code card from the slot as it may prove useful to them later.

They crept down the corridor in the direction of the exit in which they had first been brought through. Karl was lagging behind, being a little overweight from excessive indulgences.

Neville stopped to help him, but when they got to the end of the corridor, Belinda and Tito were nowhere in sight.

"Oh blast!" exclaimed Neville. "We've lost them. I think—"

Neville was cut short by the sounds of gunfire a few meters away.

"Oh dear god, please let them be all right!" said Karl in a whimper. They both crouched at the corner of the corridor until the firing had ceased.

"What now?" asked Karl in a whisper.

"Take a peek around the corner and see if you can see anyone," whispered Neville. Karl nodded. He gingerly stuck his head around the corner into the next corridor and found himself staring down the muzzle of a rifle once more. The guard was standing a few inches away looking in the opposite direction but he had a radio earpiece on, so it was evident that his hearing was slightly impaired and he was unaware of their presence. He dared another look and saw at the far end of the corridor, Belinda and Tito being marshaled away by several guards.

"They've been caught again!" whispered Karl. Neville shook his head and sighed.

"Oh dear, this isn't going well at all, is it!"

"It's about to get a lot worse for you two!" said a third voice. Karl and Neville both looked up at the guard who had stood at the corner.

"UP!" he shouted as he waved his gun in an upward motion. Releasing one hand from the barrel of the rifle, he reached for the intercom device that hung from a loop on the front of his flack jacket. Before he could report that he had captured the two fugitives, Neville slumped to the floor and began wailing wildly while Karl looked on, totally confused. The guard shouted at Neville to get up, but he continued wailing uncontrollably so the guard approached him and went to push the gun in his face. As he did so, Neville lunged forward and all Karl saw a flash of silver, and the guard was sent reeling back howling wildly clutching his side. Seconds later, Neville was on his feet and had the gun in his possession. He snatched the intercom and earpiece from the fallen guard, and after a second or so of hesitation, turned his head and slammed the rifle into the side of the guard's head knocking him senseless. Karl stood there in absolute disbelief.

"Neville, what did you do?"

Neville looked back at him, his face portraying the disgust he felt for himself. "I've bought us some time Karl, that's what I've done. Now give me that scarf of yours."

Karl watched with keen interest as Neville wrapped the scarf around the guard's torso.

"It's a tourniquet, Karl. I can't let the poor brute bleed to death, can I!" added Neville.

Chapter 9

Darkness Falls

"That's quite a temper you got there, missy!" said Marcus Deveraux as he laughed and circled Belinda, who was once more tied to her seat. Belinda didn't even look at him. She sat there with her eyes fixed on the floor, but that didn't prevent her from knowing how close Deveraux was getting due to the vile scent of charred tobacco and stale body odor.

She flinched as she felt one fat, sweaty hand grip her chin and force her head upward to come level with those sinister pig-like eyes and that bulbous crimson nose.

"What am Ah gonna do with y'all? You gonna keep pestering me until Ah give up and play nice?"

Belinda glared at him. "Go to hell you bastard!" she spat back at him.

"WOWEE, Did ya hear that, Reichstein? She gone and damned me to hell!"

The battered and somewhat crestfallen Reichstein sniggered and then winced at the pain from smiling. "Why don't you just kill us and be done with it, you pig!" snapped Belinda.

This statement took Deveraux aback.

"Kill you? What ever gave you that idea?"

Belinda realized that that was not his intention after all.

"I may be many things, missy, but Ah is not a MURDERER!"

Tito was in another room adjacent to the one in which Belinda was in. She could hear him cursing and swearing as several guards were beating him up.

"Leave him alone!" she cried.

"Oh, now you're making demands of me!" He stood up and gave a nod to one guard nearest the door and moments later the sounds had ceased.

"Is there anything else Ah can do for you, missy?"

Belinda looked up at him and smiled a sarcastic smile. "Firstly, stop calling me 'missy,' and secondly, you can untie me, give me an iron bar and let me beat that ugly shit-filled head of yours to a pulp!"

Deveraux slammed his fat hands onto the chair arms and came centimeters from her face.

"You don't get it do ya! Ah need you and your little band of do-gooders to stay outta my way. I'm on to something really big here, and Ah don't need you poking your god damn hooters in where they isn't wanted!"

Belinda recoiled as best she could from the smell of the fat man's fetid breath.

"I'm an archeologist, not Sherlock bloody Holmes, you thick sod!" Belinda spat back at him. Deveraux stood up and stepped back from her. He had a blank expression on his face for a few seconds and then he began to roar with laughter.

"You still don't get it, do you?" he bellowed as he wiped the sweat from his brow with his sleeve.

"You think this is all about findin' some dusty ol' relics in the dirt out there? You're more stupid than I thought!"

"Don't call me stupid!" shouted Belinda

"Oh, and what are you gonna do about it, MISSY?" teased

Deveraux. "Now what was it? Oh yeah, beat my ugly, shit-filled head to a pulp?" Deveraux laughed some more before turning to walk away from her.

"Take 'em down to the lower levels and, Wilhelm—lock 'em up tight this time!" Wilhelm Reichstein muttered something under his breath and sneered at Deveraux when he was sure he wasn't looking.

"Oh, and Wilhelm, can you do me one tiny favor please?" Reichstein knew this was going to end in him being shouted at in front of all the guards.

"Yes, Heir Deveraux?"

Deveraux spun around, his eyes aflame, his face scarlet and the little veins on the sides of his head looking like they were going to rupture at any moment.

"FIND WESTON AND WITT, LOCK 'EM UP WITH THESE TWO, AND IF YOU EVER BACKCHAT ME AGAIN, I'LL FEED YOUR SORRY YELLER ASS TO THE VULTURES, GOT IT?" Deveraux bellowed, showering him with saliva. Reichstein, as before, seemed unfazed by the boiling, seething bulk in front of him.

"I will do as you wish, mien heir." And with that he turned and nodded at two guards to get Belinda and Tito and left the room with the remaining guards behind him.

"Karl, where are we going?" asked Neville as the two men skulked slowly along a dimly lit passageway. "Were going to stop Deveraux and rescue Belinda and Tito!"

Neville winced at the idea of himself as a hero. He hated handling babies and washing the dog, he was no hero.

"Um, might I make an observation here?" said Neville sheepishly.

Karl stopped dead in his tracks. "What is it? You're not scared are you? After all, you are the one with the rifle, aren't you?"

Neville realized that Karl was right and thrust the weapon into Karl's hands.

"You take it! You have more gusto than me anyhow, Karl."

Karl huffed before rubbing his chin, which he often did when he was thinking hard. "Let's go in here out of the way and think of a way to throw a spanner in Deveraux's works."

They entered a room to the left of the passageway using the pass card that Neville had acquired. As they entered, Karl had his head bent down, deep in thought so he didn't notice that Neville had stopped just inside until he walked into the back of him

"Neville, I do wish you wouldn't just stop like tha—GOOD LORD!"

Karl now saw why Neville had stopped dead in his tracks. The had evidently walked into a viewing gallery that overlooked a hangar-style room in which the two helicopters were that they had seen before they were captured, and in the middle of the floor of the hangar was the huge black wedge-shaped craft they had seen slowly gliding across the plain. There seemed to be an immense amount of activity going on around the wedge-shaped craft. Karl was straining to see as far forward as possible, and to his surprise Neville wasn't holding him back because he was also attempting to gain a better view from this cramped little gallery. As they watched, they observed two figures emerge from the wedge. Both were dressed in flight suits and Neville was a little disappointed that there was absolutely nothing remotely alien about the pilots of this mysterious craft. As they watched, Karl had the distinct feeling that they too were being watched. Sure enough, down on the main hangar deck, stood an ape-like burly man with a shock of bright ginger hair staring up at the gallery. Karl wasn't sure if they had been observed, so he backed slowly away from the plate glass window. Neville, observing Karl's actions, did the same, but as he did so, he felt something jab into his back. Immediately he put his hands up in surrender. Karl saw what he was doing and started to giggle like a child. Neville, realizing that Karl had found something highly amusing, turned his head to see that he had backed into a fire extinguisher right next to the door. It was then that they both saw it.

Next to the extinguisher, muted to the same drab colors as the walls around it was a big junction box. Neville opened the door of the box and grinned. Karl saw him smiling and peered into the box, He too began to grin. Inside the box was a large red priming handle and a trip switch over which was a plate color coded in black and yellow chevrons which read "MAIN POWER LINE. DO NOT DISCONNECT."

"I think we have just found our 'spanner,' Karl," said Neville with a distinctly mischievous tone. Together they broke off the plate and pulled done on the primer handle then Neville went to flip the trip switch but hesitated.

"Well? Flip it then," said Karl.

"No," said Neville. "This was your plan, you should do it. After all, when we finally encounter that oafish buffoon Deveraux again, you can take the credit for it!"

Karl nodded. "Excellent idea, Neville!" And with that, he flicked the switch and everything went pitch black. The only sounds were that of a few electric turbines whining down as they lost power.

"Maybe we should have found some torches first?" said Neville jovially. Karl could be heard to huff in the darkness. He gingerly took a few paces forward and heard a clunk as something heavy hit the floor behind him and suddenly there was a golden shaft of light spilling out from an object on the floor. "Look Karl, that guns got a torch on the end!" The beam of light waved this way and that as Karl stumbled to pick it up but kicked it twice in the attempt. It appeared that the light show could be observed from the lower decks of the hangar because both Neville and Karl could hear a commotion of voices from below them and people cursing as the fell over each other and stumbled into things.

"I think we had better leave before we draw any more attention to ourselves," said Karl. Neville nodded and then realized that Karl couldn't see him.

"Um, yes indeed. Good idea, Karl," he responded. Karl picked up the gun and they proceeded to cautiously leave the gallery and return into the corridor beyond. To their surprise, there were emergency lights in place at regular intervals along the corridor which afforded them a little light, even if it was an eerie electric blue that made the shadows stretch and contort into weird shapes and the corners were as black as pitch. "Which way?" asked Karl. Neville was thinking hard.

"I think we came down three rights and two lefts," he said after a minute or so.

"I doubt very much that Belinda and Tito would have been taken back to that little cell. They could be anywhere, and we don't t know how big this place is!" Neville didn't answer. He was still deep in thought.

"I think we should head downwards," he said at last.

Karl flashed the torch in his face. "Why?" said Karl abruptly.

"There has to be some form of main entrance down on the plain. The vehicles that drove up here after us won't have gotten up the embankment to the doors we came through, and besides, there are probably some more rooms and weapons stores down below as well. What's more, I'd wager our rotund renegade, Mr. Deveraux, has sent our colleagues down below to a more secure environment."

Karl's face was just visible in the watery light. He didn't look pleased.

"More secure you say?" He swallowed hard. "Very well, on into the belly of the beast," he said.

Neville smiled weakly. "Indeed, may fortune favor the brave," he added.

"Foolish," Karl replied.

"Pardon?" said Neville.

Karl sighed. "It's 'may fortune favor the foolish.'"

Neville chuckled. "I really think you'll find it's brave, Karl."

They walked slowly through the gloom to the end of the narrow corridor muttering to each other

"I assure you that it's brave, Karl."

"Trust me, Neville, I know that it's foolish."

Slowly and cautiously, Karl and Neville made their way along the corridor until they came to a pitch-dark stairwell, and in single file, tethered together by the gun strap of the rifle, they descended into the darkness.

Chapter 10

Vertical Challenge

"Take your bloody hands off me!" shouted Belinda as she and Tito were finally released into another darkened room. Tito grunted as he landed face down on the floor, still shaking from the severe beating he had received while Deveraux was interrogating Belinda. She heard the high-pitched laugh of the weaselly Reichstein as the door slammed hard in on them. There was a moment of silence and then came the sound of a digital code being punched in followed by the clicking and whirring of a highly complex locking mechanism.

"Not such an easy way outta here this time," said Tito as he righted himself onto his buttocks and sat with his back against the wall. In the ethereal blue glow of the emergency lighting, Belinda could see the black line that ran down the side of Tito's face. She knew it was blood and felt that she could have stopped his torture far sooner than she had.

Without giving it another thought, she tore off the sleeve of her shirt and used it as a bandage to try and cleanse the wound as best as she could.

"Where do you suppose we are?" she asked him, trying to make light conversation. Tito looked around and winched as he turned a little too far.

"A storeroom, I think." He pointed behind her to a row of narrow shelves with a Spartan display of three or four boxes on them. She got up and went over to investigate, but as she approached the shelves, she kicked something that skidded across the floor with a metallic *ping*. She bent down to retrieve the object and she could hear Tito grunting as he was adjusting himself for a better look. His curiosity soon disappeared as a beam of soft, yellow light shot out from Belinda's hand.

"Well, it's a good start!" she said.

"Ouch, watch where you're going, Karl!" exclaimed Neville as he and Karl stumbled on through the darkened corridors.

"I would do that if I could see where I was going," said Karl snidely. As the two men scurried along the dark corridors of the labyrinthine sub-levels of the complex, neither of them seemed to be aware of the drumming noise that was steadily getting louder as they went deeper and deeper, until Neville finally exclaimed that he felt rather than heard the drumming.

The two men paused in the corridor for a moment or two, and just as they were planning to push on, Neville gasped and Karl squealed with shock as the power was restored and the corridor burst into white light.

In their new prison, Belinda and Tito were still in near darkness.

"I wish I could make out what was in these boxes," she said. The torch was dying rapidly as she realized all too late that all the light she had was simply residual charge left from the now-spent batteries.

"Power still out?" asked Tito

"Yep, looks like it," said Belinda. And then it dawned on her. If the power was out, how had Reichstein managed to lock the door?

She went quickly over to the door and studied the electronic panel with the last dying rays from the torch. From the gray junction box on the wall, she followed the cable up to the ceiling and through a grate that led somewhere, somewhere away from here. Between them, now that Tito had regained a little of his strength, they managed to move one of the lightweight shelves across the room to beneath the grate, and Belinda scrambled up and examined it in the eerie blue twilight.

"I think I can get it open," she said as she fumbled about with catches. Then, with a metallic, noisy rattle, the grate came loose, fell from her grip and smacked Tito squarely on the head. He fell to the floor with a thud and began muttering the strongest profanities imaginable through gritted teeth.

"Shit! Sorry!" said Belinda apologetically whilst trying hard not to giggle.

Tito stood up, rubbing his head. "Can you get through?" he asked impatiently.

"I think so," Belinda answered as she pulled her arm back out of the cavity. "Where to go though is the most important question," she answered. Tito grumbled under his breath.

"Anywhere away from here would be good!" he said sharply.

Belinda gave him a sheepish smile and then half her body disappeared up into the cavity in the ceiling. It was a tight squeeze in the conduit amid all the power cables and plumbing, but the blue light was brighter up here and she could see that there was an air duct about thirty yards ahead of her with an opening in it. This would serve as their escape route before deciding how to track down Neville and Karl. Within minutes, both Tito and Belinda were crammed up inside the conduit preparing to press on once Tito had reattached the grate to the fixings in the ceiling to buy some time when their captors realized they had escaped.

It was hard going as they pushed on, and Belinda winced every time she scratched her arm or leg on cable ties and metal plates, but they finally reached the air vent and soon they were inside it. It was only a short drop to the bottom, but then they looked up and saw that the chimney-like vent towered away into the darkness above them.

Karl and Neville had holed up in an alcove when they heard voices coming from the end of the long corridor that they were cautiously pressing down and had so far seen no one.

"Where do you suppose they are?" inquired Neville quietly.

"Bear with me, I'll just consult my crystal ball, shall I?" Karl sarcastically replied. Neville looked down at him over the top of his glasses.

"Sarcasm is the lowest form of wit, you know."

Karl chuckled. "No pun intended there I hope!" Karl was about to say something else when Neville slapped a hand across his mouth.

"Listen," he said in a whisper. They both strained to hear over the monotonous drown of electrical equipment thumping in the walls around them.

"If I'm not mistaken, that sounds like a woman's voice." Sure enough they could just make the exasperated ravings of an irritated female.

"Belinda!" they said in unison.

Behind them in the alcove was a service hatch, haphazardly fixed with a couple of dirty wing nuts. Neville removed the panel, and Karl stuck his head through into a dark vent.

"I can't see a blessed thing! Pass me the torch, would you?" Neville handed him the gun light and he thrust his head into the vent again. This time he switched on the torch and a beam of yellow light cascaded down the shaft.

"Yoohoo, anyone down there?" called Karl.

Far below in the diminishing light from the torch, he could just make out the flushed and irritated features of Belinda and the grim set features of Tito.

After brief and utterly pointless conversation down the shaft, Belinda told Karl in an extremely colorful manner to find a way for them to ascend the shaft and quickly. But as Karl retracted his head and looked at Neville, he was quite flushed.

"Is she all right, what did she say?" asked Neville.

"I don't care to repeat what she said to me; suffice to say we need to find rope or other climbing implement to get them out of there."

Neville looked around the alcove. There was nothing. He stuck his head into the corridor and a thought struck him. There must be miles and miles of insulated ducting in the very walls that surrounded them. "Karl, be a gent and lend a hand getting this other panel off would you!"

Karl looked puzzled for a moment and then grinned broadly as together they managed to prize the second panel off the wall. Sure enough, there were an assortment of cables, wires and tubes in the wall cavity. Karl went straight for the first cable he saw, but Neville blocked him before he could grab it.

"Do you want to fry them or rescue them? That's a live power cable!" Neville turned around and examined the selection of cables leaving the scolded Karl to stand, vacant with that characteristic heavy frown of his.

Neville finally identified a data cable and using his penknife; he slit the casing and began to pull the cable through. A while later, after extracting as much lax cable as possible, Karl signaled to Belinda and Tito with torch and seconds later, they dumped one end of the cable through the service opening.

Below, Belinda and Tito heard the clatter and whipping sound of the cable falling down the shaft and as the sound got closer, Belinda realized that there was a lot of cable coming their way. She instantly backed against the side of the shaft and warned Tito to do the same, but being somewhat dazed from recent events, Tito didn't quite register what Belinda had said and just looked inquisitively at her. His expression turned from that of curiosity to extreme pain as the last bundle of the flexible cable bounced of his head and ricocheted of the side of the shaft with a resonating clang. Tito slammed both his hands onto his head, winced and then let out the vilest string of profanities up the shaft at the faint pudgy outline of Karl, who withdrew his head and a moment later was replaced with Neville.

"Sorry! My fault," he called down the shaft.

No cognitive response was audible, just some grunts and growls from the bruised and battered Tito. Soon, Belinda and Tito were clambering up the cable, which was no easy task as it was strong but very slim and made footholds on it very difficult. Belinda made Tito go first and she followed painfully slowly up the cable. Karl and Neville were too engrossed in monitoring the tensile strength of the cable and watching the progress of the two intrepid climbers to notice the uniform drumming of several pairs of feet heading their way. Tito was first out of the shaft and Belinda followed a moment later. They all collapsed in a heap and rested for a moment before Belinda noticed the footfalls that were fast approaching.

"What now?" she moaned.

Tito, despite sustaining several injuries to his head was still thinking fast. He snatched the gun out of Neville's grip and pointed it at the sprinkler sensor in the ceiling above them. One shot hit home with a *ting*, and instantly they were all doused in freezing water.

Belinda and Karl both gasped as the icy water soaked them to the skin but there was no time for physical discomfort. Tito was already up, albeit a touch rickety on his feet, and he quickly led the rest of them down the corridor in the direction of the footfalls, which were barely audible over the hissing of the water. A moment later, they had ducked into a service corridor and burst through the first door they came to. After they had taken a few seconds to collect themselves, they took in their new surroundings. Behind them, the sound of splashing and fizzing water ceased as the sprinkler system shut off but that was followed by a loud 'clunk' as the door locked behind them.

"Shit!" cursed Belinda.

"Evidently, the doors are designed to unlock in the event of a fire and relock after the emergency is over," added Neville

"Thanks, Einstein!" spat Belinda with definitive sharpness in her tone.

They had, they now realized, run into a large, dry darkened room apparently unaffected by the fire system with the exception of the door.

Tito led them across the room and cursed as he walked into a large obstacle in the middle of the room. He slowly navigated his way around it and made his way over to the opposite corner where in the gloom he could make out the shape of what appeared to be cargo boxes or crates. Either way, it was a good place to hide for now. Belinda, Neville and Karl followed suit and they all collapsed on the floor, catching their breath before planning their next course of action.

The Cerebratome

Chapter 11

A moment later, they heard a commotion outside and a lot of raised voices, including that of Marcus Deveraux.

"He won't be best pleased if he finds us now," remarked Neville

"Screw him!" said Belinda as she shifted awkwardly in the cramped space. Tito sat nursing a bruised head, sore palms and now a severely bruised hip.

"What the hell did you walk into, Tito?" Belinda asked.

Tito shrugged and then realized that Belinda probably couldn't see the gesture. "Beats me!" he said. "It was bloody big and hard, I know that much!" he said as he continued to rub his injuries in a vain effort to ease the discomfort.

"Are you okay, Karl?" Belinda asked.

"Hmm, oh yes I'm fine, just a little soggy around the edges but otherwise okay, thank you." Neville quietly got to his feet and pulled the torch from his pocket.

"What are you doing, Neville?" asked Belinda, slightly concerned.

"Just taking a peek, my dear," he said as he gingerly stepped out from behind the crates and switched on the torch. Instantly the white beam of light cascaded down onto the circular object that Tito had stumbled against. Neville gasped, and the other three, hearing his exclamation, froze in fear. For a moment they thought they had been discovered but when no other noise followed Neville's exclamation Belinda and Karl rose to follow him.

When they emerged from behind the crates, they saw Neville standing still, apparently in awe of the object before him. They quietly approached him and Neville was beginning to giggle like a child. "Is this what I think it is, Karl?" he said with an excitement.

"I think it could well be, Neville," replied Karl, not taking his eyes of the thing for an instant.

"What is it?" asked Belinda with a look of childish wonder in her eyes.

"That, my dear Belinda, could well be the Cerebratome!"

Sitting on the floor in front of them, bathed in the light from the torch, was the most bizarre object Belinda had ever seen. The Cerebratome was a huge circular dais raised upon a heavy pedestal that was roughly four feet in height and nearly twelve feet across. Around the circumference of the object at regular intervals were thirteen depressed sockets; the center rose up into a kind of small platform upon which was a complex metallic arrangement of rings and spheres of various sizes. The whole thing was filthy and Belinda knew at once that this object, whatever it was, had only recently been excavated from the earth after god only knew how long.

"Karl, humor me just once and please pretend that I have absolutely no idea what you're talking about," said Belinda sarcastically.

Karl did the usual thing when he was spoken to in a stern voice; he looked at Belinda and cocked his head like a scorned puppy.

"Very well, my dear, I will tell you all I know. Neville, I may need your expertise along the way." Neville nodded and followed Karl with the torch as he strolled, Hitchcock-style around the stone dais.

"If I am correct, then this is the Cerebratome. As far as I can ascertain from the information that was made available to me, it is a book."

Belinda looked even more puzzled than before.

"One might say a library to be more exact. Legend has it that the Cerebratome held the combined knowledge of the universe and that only those with, shall we say 'the right redeeming qualities' would be permitted to view its contents. I really had no idea we would stumble on to the whole thing quite like this. I mean, I myself have read passages about such a device, but it's believed to be nothing more than a myth! Deveraux must have some extremely accurate data to procure such facilities as these and in addition, know exactly where to unearth this miraculous relic!"

Just then they heard a noise in the corridor outside.

"Quick, hide!" whispered Belinda.

Neville and Belinda bolted for the safety of the crates where Tito still sat, but Karl had managed to stumble and trip over as the door handle was being depressed. He quickly bolted upright and spun to face the door, which by this time was now just about to open as he could see thin rods of light filtering through the frame, and then the door opened. A split second later, in walked Wilhelm Reichstein. His eyes took a few seconds to adjust to the gloom in the room, and due to this fact; he failed to see a dumpy fat man in a filthy linen suit drop down behind the Cerebratome, out of sight.

Karl heard him grumbling to himself about no lights, Deveraux and the guards. Karl shifted around on the floor to keep the stone dais between him and Reichstein who, he noticed, had a rifle slung haphazardly across his left shoulder.

He walked over to the crates, and for a second, Karl's heart jumped into his mouth because he feared that the other three might give away their position.

Evidently Wilhelm was too preoccupied with his personal ranting to notice four sets of haphazard wet footprints on the floor beside him.

He worried at the crates for a moment perhaps, removed the item he was after and headed for the open door. Before leaving, Karl clearly heard the German bark an order into his radio to get Pullman down to the dais room to start cleanup on this thing. The reply was "Ten minutes, sir."

Reichstein huffed, grumbled a bit more and walked out the door, which promptly locked itself again behind him.

Karl gave a sigh of relief as he bolted over to the crates as fast as he could.

"We have precisely ten minutes to get out of here before more people arrive again!" he squeaked with worry.

"Someone called 'Pullman' is on his way!"

Belinda was about to speak when Neville interrupted. "Her way," he said with a stone cold voice.

"Pardon?" quizzed Karl.

"Pullman is a she. SHE is on HER way," he added, still in the unfamiliar cold voice.

Neville was suddenly aware that he had the full and undivided attention of three pairs of eyes, which belonged top three very curious people.

Neville gulped and gave a sheepish half-smile.

Chapter 12
An Unexpected Reunion

Belinda was the first to break the inquisitive silence "Something you'd like to share with us, Neville?" she ordered rather than said.

Tito just sat; still tending his wounds while Karl had the expression of a child waiting for the hilarious punch line of a schoolyard joke.

"Madeline Pullman was my research partner when we were both working for the French government approximately three years ago."

Karl sagged a little.

"Did you know she was in league with Deveraux by any chance, or were you planning on a little surprise reunion?" Karl said with an air sarcasm that wholly unsuited him.

"No. Well, sort of. I had an idea that she may be out here in this part of the world but I had no idea that she might be working for Deveraux."

Karl sighed. "Maybe it's a different Pullman then?"

Belinda shot him a frosty glare. "Karl, we are in a secret

installation in the middle of darkest Peru. How many Pullmans do you honestly think there are in a place like this?"

Karl gave the puppy look again. "Maybe you have a point, my dear." Then he shut up much to Tito's relief, who found Karl the most irritating of people at times, especially as he was currently holding him responsible for two of his injuries.

Neville continued. "I last heard that Madeline had annexed herself to a little quasi governmental department working as an advisor on certain historical elements of scientific…"

"We *get* the idea," interjected Belinda.

"The question is what's she doing here, and what's she's got to do with Deveraux?" Karl frowned as if deep in thought.

Neville looked over to Karl.

"You used to be affiliated with Marcus Deveraux, didn't you, Karl. Can you shed any light upon this?"

Karl looked at them and found that it was now he that was the center of attention. "Marcus Deveraux and I had a few business transactions that happened to have a common outcome, and I did partake of a few fruitful enterprises with him. That was of course before I discovered his true, capitalistic side. Money and power are all that interest that man. It was at that point of discovering this in the harshest possible way that told me to relinquish all business ties with him."

"And…" added Tito, being the first thing he had said to Karl since the incident in the vent shaft.

"It's quite probable that either this woman is being coerced and or threatened into work or is in on the promise of a hefty wage packet at the end. When it comes to convincing people to do his bidding, Marcus Deveraux could give the devil a run for his money!"

They continued discussing their options for a few more minutes before deciding how best to proceed, but as they slowly got up to try and formulate a plane of escape, Neville heard the bleeping of a numerical combination being entered on the keypad outside. Belinda was supporting Tito, whose leg was still painful, when the door started to open and they were all forced to dive for cover back behind the crates once more.

Belinda stumbled and both she and Tito when flying down with a thud and Karl, not being the most astute of people, missed his footing and went flying down on top of both of them, landing on Tito's already injured leg.

Belinda was quick enough to slap her and over his mouth before he could let forth another verbal assault at the pathetically apologetic fat man who was now cringing in the corner.

Only Neville remained standing, concealed by the line of end crates. His overwhelming curiosity was getting the better of him as he stood watching as a slim curvaceous figure strode into the room and headed for the far left wall. A moment later, the room was illuminated like a dark blind being thrown back from a window on a blazing summer's day. Neville allowed for his eyes to adjust in the dazzling light before peering again. As he did so, he gave a little sigh. Madeline was standing to the right of the Cerebratome with her blonde hair tied back in a bun and the quintessential thin horn-rimmed glasses perched at the tip of her petite nose. At this point Belinda noticed Karl trying to scramble up as quickly and quietly as he could with one arm outstretched in an attempt to grab Neville's shirt. Belinda and Tito looked on in horror as Karl failed to secure a grip and fell flat on his pudgy face and allowed Neville to stroll straight out from behind the crates.

"What the hell is he doing?" hissed Belinda. They heard him take a few steps forwards and stop.

"Hello, Madeline."

Madeline gave a cry of shock and surprise when she realized she was not alone in the room.

"Neville, Neville Whitt, is that you?" Neville walked over to her. In his eyes she was still as radiant as ever.

"Madeline, what are you doing here?"

Madeline gave a little laugh. "I think I should be the one asking you that question."

Neville smirked and brushed some of his silvery hair away from his face. "I'm here under the duress of Marcus Deveraux."

Madeline looked at him over the horn-rimmed glasses like an agitated schoolmistress. "Am I addressing the same Neville Whitt from Oxford who doesn't like hot places, hates foreign food and generally hates to travel? And here I find you in a disheveled state in the bowels of a secret research complex in heart of Peru as a guest of Mr. Deveraux, alone. I sincerely doubt it."

She glared at him.

"Why are you really here, Neville?" Neville cleared his throat and called to Belinda, Tito and Karl to come out. Madeline looked over to the crates from where Neville had appeared and was a little surprised to see a young, athletic woman, a middle-aged Latin American (who was evidently sporting a few injuries) and a short, rotund man with messy black hair walk gingerly out from their hiding place.

Madeline looked a little shocked at the quartet that now stood before her.

"I'd like to say it's a pleasant surprise to see you, Madeline, but after the way we left things back in Oxford, well. You don't exactly deserve my hand of friendship do you?"

Karl and Belinda looked at each other with curiosity and Karl gave a little shrug. Neville was about to say something else but he could see that Madeline was turning red with anger. Madeline slapped him across the face and Neville recoiled from the blow that stung the left side of his face.

"I did deserve something I suppose, but that wasn't exactly what I had in mind, my dear," he said with a trace of contempt in his voice.

"How DARE you!" she spat. "You left me no choice! When funding dried up, you simply upped and left without as much as a goodbye. Did you expect me to follow you to ask for your permission to file for the same grant that you were after?"

She looked more hurt now than angry.

"I had to find some way of funding the department after you vanished like that!" Neville was beginning to portray signs of guilt and it didn't exactly make the rest of them feel comfortable as spectators in some private feud.

"I'm sorry, Madeline," Neville finally said.

He gave her a sheepish smile and tried to look as innocent and vulnerable as possible.

Madeline simply stared at him with such coldness that even Karl felt a shiver down his spine.

"Well, we should be thankful for small mercies, at least you're alright."

Then followed the most uncomfortably pregnant pause imaginable until Tito finally broke the silence

"What abouta Deveraux? Why are you working for him here?"

Madeline looked at Tito and for the first time took notice of the well built if not particularly youthful man addressing her. "It's a long story," she said .

"Look, I can see that you evidently don't want to be discovered so I would suggest that you return to your hiding place for now, because I have to get on with my assignment and no doubt, Mr. Deveraux will be here shortly." She haphazardly straightened her lab coat with one hand.

"I may not be particularly fond of you at the moment, but I like Marcus Deveraux considerably less. You really ought to try and get out of here at your earliest convenience."

Even as she spoke there came the clatter of feet from the corridor outside.

"Quick! Go and hide!"

Without having to be told twice, the four darted back to the seclusion of their crate hideout.

The door swung open and in stomped Marcus Deveraux, Wilhelm Reichstein and two guards.

"Ah, Miss Pullman, hard at work Ah see!"

The man's porcine features seemed even more prominent in the artificial light.

Marcus grinned at her with those yellow teeth which made her feel quite ill.

"Hold on what your doing here, this here doohickey's bein' moved ASAP."

Madeline looked a little confused.

"Where to? I haven't even started examining it yet!" she retorted.

Marcus's grin grew even broader. "Y'all see soon enough! Oh, and by the way, If you see anyone snoopin' around down here, you tell me immediately, ya hear?"

Madeline grinned back at him. "Oh, dear Marcus, somebody not playing by your rules?"

The grin fell from the fat mans jowls instantly. "Just remember!" he spat. "I hold the ace card here, so you'll be wise not to piss me off! Get this thing ready to transport. We move out in 2 hours!"

With that he spun around and marched away, looking notably redder than before with the guards in tow.

Wilhelm, however, stood opposite her with the Cerebratome between them, and he was fixing a most curious stare upon her.

"Lonely place out there, you know. Nothing around but plains and mountains and I dare say that one wouldn't survive very long without provisions."

Now Madeline was seeing red. "Are you threatening me?"

Reichstein recoiled theatrically at the remark. "Me? Why no, Miss Pullman. Just consider it a friendly warning." She started towards him but stopped when she saw that he was stroking the barrel of a pistol he had concealed within his grasp.

She proceeded to slowly walk up to him, stopped within a few centimeters and looked down at his groin.

"Compensating for something, are we?" she said in a sultry tone before continuing past him to the door. She physically felt the weaselly German wince at the comment.

Attacking the male ego was one weapon she knew how to use well.

A minute or so later, Belinda risked a peek and discovered that the room was now empty. She instructed the others to follow her and made it clear that now was the prime opportunity to formulate a way to escape from the complex and get help because they believed now, more than ever, that they would need it.

Chapter 13

In Transit

Within minutes, the foursome was out in the center of the room by the Cerebratome.

Belinda was thinking hard of a way to escape the complex while Tito and Neville were throwing in random, crazy ideas of escape.

Karl stood quietly by, his eyes transfixed on the dirt-encrusted relic that sat before them.

"I've got it!" he suddenly exclaimed. Neville and Tito stopped chattering in an instant and looked at him. Tito still had his arms in the air in a wildly gesticulating manner.

Belinda, still with hand on her chin was the first to speak

"Okay, what's your plan, Karl?" Karl clasped his hands behind his back and rocked slowly on the balls of his feet, which he tended to do when he was about to talk in a manner customary of a lecturer to his students. "We have very little time before this complex is crawling with personnel, and lest we forget that some of them will be here to pack the artifact up for transport."

Tito lowered his arms and opened his mouth to speak, but Belinda beat him to it.

"Would it be too much of an inconvenience for you to get to bloody point?" she said in a highly agitated tone.

"What? Oh yes, sorry. Well, we help Marcus Deveraux by packing up the Cerebratome for him!"

Karl stepped back from the Cerebratome and pointed to the floor. Up to this point, no one had noticed that the artifact stood on a large wooden square that formed the base of a packing crate.

"We simply package up the artifact with ourselves along with it! That way we are sure to discover the ultimate intentions of Deveraux and Reichstein before we inform any authority!" Tito's face dropped and Neville looked gob-smacked.

"That's your brilliant idea, Karl?" said Belinda finally.

"Well, has anyone else got a better idea?" he added. The silence affirmed that no one did. After a short time of uneasy silence, Belinda and Neville set about gathering up the remaining five panels of the crate while Tito and Karl searched for rudimentary equipment such as a good hammer and some long nails, which they found after some frantic searching. They eventually finished the four side panels encasing the Cerebratome before finally sealing themselves inside by nailing the top panel into position from within.

Had anyone been in the room at the time, they would have probably been surprised to hear a series of dull thuds, a muffled voice telling someone else to be careful and then a sharp squeal of pain followed by a colorful burst of profanities in a distinctly Mexican accent.

In the musty darkness, Neville was the first to break the silence.

"One question, Karl, what happens when they open the crate at its final destination and they see us in here with the Cerebratome?" Karl could be heard quietly chuckling to himself

"We escape from the crate before they reach their destination!" Suddenly there was a sharp ringing sound of metal on stone.

"Whata was that?" asked Tito with surprise.

"Crowbar!" said Karl with a giggle. Belinda knew that even

though she couldn't see him, Karl was grinning like the proverbial Cheshire cat in the darkness.

After what seemed an interminable time, voices were clearly heard as unseen people entered the room. Neville instantly recognized the voice of Madeline and then the heated debate between two men over who had prepared the Cerebratome for transport. Karl giggled quietly to himself but Belinda lashed out in the darkness and caught him on the forearm. The giggling ceased abruptly and was replaced by faint whispers of concern as the unseen Karl Weston fidgeted uneasily in his cramped position. The confused voices outside finally faded away and they all breathed a sigh of relief, all except Karl.

"What the hell is wrong with you, Karl?" whispered Belinda

"I must apologize in advance for what I'm about to do!" replied Karl. But before Belinda could answer him there was a sound like air being rapidly let out of a balloon immediately followed by a methane twang in the air.

Neville managed to stifle a cough as they heard the doors open followed by some raised voices and a parade of footsteps.

Moments later the crate rocked as it was struck from the side with a violent thud followed by more raised voices, and then after a short time, there was a gentle jolt and the sensation of movement indicated by a slight swing told them that they were on their way. By this time, Tito had managed to poke a knot out of one panel and was sucking in a great lungful of Weston-free air.

They must have been swaying for about ten minutes or so because Belinda was beginning to feel a little queasy from the motion, but her symptoms were quickly alleviated when they came down with a hard bump. Neville slipped from his perch on the edge of the Cerebratome and banged his shin so hard that he yelped in pain, which made the others freeze in apprehension, but it appeared that anyone outside was either out of earshot or distracted with some other duty.

After a few minutes or so, Tito gave a huge sigh of relief before shooting Neville an evil stare, the kind of stare that told you that "If we get out of this alive, you'll have to worry what I'll do to you!"

Belinda shuffled over to the knot hole in the wood and gingerly peered out. They had evidently been transported up to the main entrance that they had seen the black wedge fly into when they first arrived on the plateau. In the distance were Wilhelm Reichstein and Marcus Deveraux. They were stood near the hangar-style doors and Marcus was talking, or rather shouting, at Madeline about something. Belinda could see her cool expressionless face absorbing the ranting onslaught from Deveraux. Soon after, they walked over to a black jeep and clambered in. Belinda could see the Quetzaquoatl emblem on the side, and as she was mulling over how someone as disreputable as Deveraux could get any sort of government funding and put it down to a rather thin and unimaginative cover story, the doors in front of them parted and the daylight poured in, which made Belinda wince. She'd forgotten how long it had been since she had seen daylight.

Come to think of it, how long had they been down here in this labyrinth running away from this vulgar fat man and his weasely cohort? Suddenly, her vision was obscured by a blanket of green, and a plastic rustling sound told her that the crate was being covered with a tarpaulin prior to transport.

A jolt came and she was thrown backwards onto Karl and Neville. The crate beneath them began to tremble, the distinctive smell of burning diesel soon became present and with another jolt, they were set in motion, jerkily at first but soon a smooth ride was to be had by the unseen hitchhikers.

After what seemed an interminable time, Karl got up, and steadying himself with one hand on the side of the crate, made his way to the opposite corner where Tito sat. He knew he had reached him when he took one step too many and his foot struck something soft which was followed by a whine of pain from Tito.

"Sorry!" whispered Karl.

"You don't have to whisper. The wind alone agitating the tarpaulin will make us totally inaudible," said Neville.

"Yeah, and they can't hear us either," added Belinda. Tito had stood up and was about to let out some seriously pent up anger against Karl when there was a violent jolt and he was flung backwards. As he did so, his fist made contact with something that felt satisfyingly like a face. There was a moment's pause, and Tito had recovered his balance and retrieved the crowbar. With this in hand, he set to work loosening some of the individual planks that made up one side of the crate.

After some minutes jostling with the crowbar and fighting to keep his balance, Tito had finally loosened enough planks to afford a gap large enough to crawl through. And so, one by one they proceeded to crawl out of the crate and onto the trailer of a large truck. As luck would have it, the tarpaulin was tied down in such a way that it acted as an awning to allow the escape from the crate to be unobserved by any outsiders. At last they were all out, and Tito did his best to replace the planks while Belinda attempted to work out where they were headed. Neville was busy trying to make himself as presentable as possible when he saw Karl nursing a black eye.

"What happened to you?" inquired Neville.

"I think I fell against something with that last jolt."

Neville looked at Tito and saw that he was grinning like a schoolboy. "It was an accident!" he said and raised an empty palm skywards. Neville couldn't hold back a thin smile.

Belinda was in the process of working her way around the crate in order to ascertain their orientation on the trailer. She bent down and gingerly peered from beneath the tarpaulin and saw that they had crawled from the side of the crate nearest the rear of the truck. She could see some yards off the rest of the convoy in transit. There were at least seven other vehicles behind them, including one that looked identical to the one they were traveling on with the exception that this had a tarpaulin that quite obviously was covering something infinitely larger than a crate, something large and broad and wedge-shaped.

A second heavy jolt nearly sent her out from beneath the tarpaulin and she gripped it for dear life and did her best to regain her balance. She soon rejoined the others by the side of the crate.

"We're on the left side of the truck." She consulted her GPS watch. "Traveling east," she added.

They all looked at Tito.

"Any ideas as to our heading?" asked Neville.

Tito thought for a moment before saying that he had a vague idea that there were a range of mountains to the east, some that had huge caverns in them. "It would make a good hidey-place," he added.

"What did you see, Belinda?" asked Karl, still nursing his black eye.

"We're part of a convoy. There are at least seven vehicles behind us and maybe just as many in front and..." Her sentence trailed off.

"And?" asked Neville.

"And on the trailer a few trucks back, there's a massive wedge shaped object."

Neville, Tito and Karl all looked at one another.

"Something I should know?" asked Belinda.

Karl spoke up first. "When we headed up to the complex we made our way up onto a rise where we saw..." He paused, took a deep breath, and said "We saw a UFO, and it was wedge-shaped." Neville nodded in agreement, and Tito gave Belinda the look that told her that what was said was true. Karl was getting a little hot under the collar.

"There is no way on God's green earth that Marcus Deveraux has managed all this on government funding and aid from the Peruvian authorities. He's obviously using that as a cover story."

As they traveled, Belinda, Tito and Neville listened as Karl recounted memories of when he and Deveraux had been business associates and that he had often referred to Karl for information regarding antiquities.

"He knows as much about these skulls as I do about flying a plane!"

"So what's his purpose here then?" asked Belinda.

"My theory," said Neville, "is that it has something to do with that frightful German chap. I think that Deveraux has the hired muscle that Reichstein needs but ultimately not even Deveraux is in full possession of the facts surrounding this mystery."

Suddenly, a thunderous shock sent them all flying to one side and Neville was pitched onto Karl, who was very nearly was thrown out from beneath the tarp. Had it not been for Tito acting like lightning and grabbing his collar, he would have been. They all scrambled back to the limited safety of the crate when Belinda suggested that they move around to the other side of the crate so that they were positioned behind the cab of the truck. Tito nodded.

"Right, we might be able to see where were going."

"You're quiet, ma dear," said Deveraux as he puffed on a huge, rancid smelling cigar. Madeline sat in between the fat, sweaty bulk of Marcus Deveraux and the snide, weasel-like form of Wilhelm Reichstein as they rode in the back of the jeep across the dusty plain.

"Do you really have to pollute the air with that filth? God only knows that your body odor is enough to knock out an elephant!"

Deveraux nearly choked on a puff from the cigar as Reichstein laughed, which showed Madeline that even the cold, calculating German had the beginnings of a sense of humor. Deveraux composed himself after a series of whopping coughs that spattered the driver's neck with saliva.

"Who the hell do ya think y'all talking to, you jumped-up little floozy! One more remark like that and you know what the consequences will be! And that ain't any idle threat!"

Madeline seemed a little shaken from the verbal onslaught but she fought to keep her composure.

The guard in the passenger seat was speaking into the crackling radio, and a moment later he turned to Marcus.

"Sir, base one reports a clean sweep. There's no sign of the prisoners."

Marcus grunted, snatched the radio from the guard's hand and twisted the knob on the radio to change the frequency. "All units, this is Deveraux. We have intruders onboard the convoy. Ah repeat we have intruders onboard the convoy. Stop and search your vehicles. If you find anyone, disable them if you have to, but I want them alive!"

One by one, the procession of vehicles ground to a halt on the dry, sun-baked plateau ,but due to the size and sheer inertia of the two transporters, one had stopped and jackknifed a little, and the other very nearly careened into it but it avoided a collision and scraped the side of it with the sound of grinding metal. Neville recoiled with horror as he saw the huge silhouette of the other truck loom up until it was almost upon them. With a violent shudder, the truck scraped against the side, causing Karl to lose his balance and Tito to stumble on top of him. Then all was still other than the clinking sound of cooling engines and the faintly audible agitated voices of drivers.

"What do you think is going on, Belinda?" asked Karl with some concern.

"I'm not sure, but if we're not moving, we're not safe. Stay as quiet as you can, I'm gonna take a look outside. Try not to move about if you can help it."

Neville and Tito shifted into a seated position with their backs to the crate while Karl stood next to them. Belinda, on hands and knees, crept towards the far side of the trailer. Cautiously, she lifted the tarpaulin a little and almost fell over as she recoiled in fear.

The Wedge

Chapter 14

"There's a group of guards outside and their searching the convoy!" she whispered.

Karl's screwed his face up in frustration, and Neville seemed grief stricken, but Tito just crawled quietly to the opposite side of the trailer, peeked out and then with one swift action rolled out from beneath it.

Karl and Neville looked horror-struck as he did this.

Seconds later there rang out the most cacophonous clatter of metal on metal, and abruptly Tito reappeared by rolling under the tarpaulin again.

"When I give-a the signal, follow me as quickly as you can, okay?"

The others agreed with him and Neville started to grin as he suddenly fathomed what Tito had done.

Moments later, the sound of feet crunching on the light gravel and clunking on the wood and metal was heard on the adjacent trailer as guards swarmed over it looking for the source of the noise, but after about five minutes, one of the unseen guards shouted "Clear!" and the sound of feet crunching on the light gravel came again. Belinda followed the sound from the far left, across in front of the trailer they were on and around to her near side where she had first spied the guards. Tito made a hissing noise to get their attention, and they all turned to see him give an indication that they were to follow him. And so one by one, they followed his example and quickly and quietly rolled out from under the tarpaulin of one truck, straight under the tarpaulin of the other, and just as Tito rolled under and dropped the edge, the tarpaulin on the other side of the truck carrying the crate was pulled up, and the sneering, rubicund face of Marcus Deveraux could be seen.

As before, the crate trailer was swarming with guards as they searched for the "intruders," but Neville, Karl, Belinda and Tito had made good use of their new cover by finding the darkest corner of the tarp under the large object that was being transported. Neville was breathing heavily and Belinda slapped her hand over his mouth to muffle him as she saw the silhouette of someone on the opposite trailer, someone rather thin and carrying a gun. The tarpaulin was suddenly lifted up, and from the invisible gloom of their corner; Belinda could see the rodent-like face of Wilhelm Reichstein peering in.

Nobody breathed as Reichstein turned to leave but then paused. It seemed as if he knew they were there but was waiting for them to make a movement or noise that would betray their presence. But then they heard the impatient, bellowing voice of Marcus Deveraux summoning him and they found it mildly amusing when, before retracting his head from under the tarpaulin, Reichstein made a rather good comedic impersonation of Deveraux.

The tarpaulin slapped back down and Belinda gave a quiet sigh of relief as they saw the silhouette of Reichstein fade away. After a while, Belinda realized that she still had her hand over Neville's mouth and withdrew it quickly, which made Neville jump a little.

Karl puffed out his cheeks and blew out in relief, "Quick thinking there, old bean!" as he patted Tito lightly on the back.

"Yeah, that was far too close for comfort that time!" added Belinda.

Neville jumped again at the sudden noise of the truck's engine roaring to life. Soon they were on their way again and the tarpaulin was lightly flapping at the edges, which afforded a nice little breeze to their otherwise humid, stifling hiding place. Karl was uneasily walking around the trailer when Neville called him. The distraction made Karl turn, but he continued walking and failed to see the low-slung protuberance from the cargo on this trailer, and with a thud, his head made contact and fell back with a thump and an exclamation.

"Bloody hell! Curse this damn thing!" At the remark from Karl, they realized almost in unison that up until this point, none of them had given any thought to the mysterious cargo that they were traveling with.

"This is that infernal craft we saw from the plateau isn't it?" exclaimed Neville.

"I do believe that you are correct, Neville!" replied Karl. And so, they all began to investigate the bizarre craft that Karl and Neville had seen lazily making its way through the air with a helicopter escort just prior to their capture.

Belinda was the only one not to have had a prior encounter with the wedge, and she was exploring it with considerable interest.

"Is this…a real UFO, Neville?" she asked with wonder.

"Sadly, I believe not, my dear," he replied.

"What do you mean, Neville?" asked Karl, looking decidedly crestfallen.

"If I am not mistaken, it appears to be the basic shell of a regular stealth aircraft with certain radical modifications, but I dare say that I would not be surprised to find that it utilized some extraterrestrial technology in its construction."

Tito was just standing on the spot, apparently in a state of complete awe of the object, just as he had been when he first heard about it. Belinda was working her way around the lower half of the fuselage when Karl, being accident-prone as he was, stumbled on something, possibly a loose bolt, and fell against the craft. There was a faint metallic clunk follow a hissing sound, and a panel on the side of the wedge nearest to Karl, slid down and a narrow set of metal steps slid out from a recess.

From their various positions around the craft, the four gathered at the opening and peered into the dark interior.

"I guess I must just have that magic touch," remarked Karl with a little giggle, but no one was paying any attention to him.

Neville ascended the steps and took a step over the threshold of the opening, and as his foot touched the floor, a series of electric blue lights set into the ceiling and the floor winked into life. The whole interior of the wedge slowly illuminated until it was bathed in a steely twilight glow. Tito and Belinda followed suit with Karl at the rear. The first thing Belinda noticed was the sheer calm of the interior. Outside on the trailer, they were being thrown about with the motion of the truck rumbling over the uneven ground but in there, total stillness.

Karl shot past her and Tito and headed for Neville.

"This has to be the culmination—no, the pinnacle of your scientific career!" Neville looked at Karl. He could see the sheer uncontrollable excitement in the man's eyes. He knew that to Karl, this was better than winning someone's luxury yacht in a game of cards or blowing several million on a frivolous wager.

"No, Karl, I'm afraid it's not. You see this is not a true UFO. It's made by man with the aid of extraterrestrial technology." The gleam of excitement seemed to fade from Karl's face, but Neville remedied the situation by pointing out that he was excited and this was the closest he had come to real extraterrestrial evidence.

Neville left Karl standing with Tito and Belinda as he walked over to what Neville took to be the command area of the ship. It was a ship after all, wasn't it? The question floated in his mind for a few moments and then he let it drift into the vast warehouse of intricate thoughts that occupied the major part of this remarkable man's mind.

At what was evidently the front of the wedge, there was an

arrangement of three seated positions, arranged triangular fashion, which were molded into the very fabric of the floor. Everything seemed fluid and contoured with the definitive absence of corners or edges. He resisted the urge to sit in the foremost seat but he knew that it would satisfy all his curiosities if he could at least "test drive" this miraculous vehicle.

The gentle hum of power within the craft made the hair on the back of their necks stand on end. "Neville, what do you assume is keeping the craft so still?" inquired Belinda. Neville seemed not to hear her. "Neville?" she called again. This time he snapped out of his dreamlike state and answered her.

"Sorry, I was miles away. What did you say?" Belinda repeated the question and the intellectual twinkle seemed to return to his eyes. He smiled thinly and without saying another word walked over to her, took her by the arm and walked her out of the craft and back onto the trailer.

"Look!" he said as he pointed to the large circular base of the craft. Belinda noticed for the first time that there was a gap of around a foot between the trailer and the craft.

"How in the hell is it doing that?" she asked him. Neville didn't say anything, he just picked up a loose bolt that was lying on the deck and tossed it beneath the craft. The bolt stopped immediately as it passed beneath the craft and rose an inch or more from the trailer.

"It's the simple principle of electromagnetic levitation, Belinda!" he said above the noise of the wind whipping against the sides of the tarpaulin.

They returned to the interior of the craft and Belinda quizzed him some more. Karl and Tito also came over to hear what Neville was saying.

"As you maybe aware, the earth generates a weak electromagnetic field." He was using his hands to draw imaginary schematics in the air. "It is this field that tells us which way is north on a compass. If you were to generate an electromagnetic field strong enough and keep it in opposition to the field of the earth, the force of gravity would keep you down so far, but your electromagnetic field would lift you so far that you would maintain a floating equilibrium."

Karl looked fascinated, Tito looked confused and Belinda was listening intently to every word as if she was taking part in some kind of exam.

"We have the hypothetical knowledge to accomplish this but certainly not the technical know how," he concluded.

"What I want to know is where they got hold of the technology to build this bloody thing!" retorted Karl. Tito answered him with a sing word. "Roswell."

All three of them looked at Tito in astonishment.

"Please tell me you didn't just say Roswell," said Neville with concealed excitement.

"Roswell, New Mexico," answered Tito. He went on to explain that when he was a boy growing up on his grandfather's farm just outside Roswell, his grandfather would tell him stories of how his family was the distant ancestors of "the sky people" and how one of them had fallen to earth from their kingdom in the sky.

"You realize this is quite a revelation!" said Neville.

"If this craft is indeed the culmination of years of research, then what in god's name is the likes of Deveraux doing with it?"

"That is one question I intend to find an answer to!" replied Karl. His face was set quite stern and they knew that when he looked like that, he meant it.

Belinda suddenly had disturbing thought. "What if those goes deeper than Deveraux? Who knows who else is involved. We could be getting into some serious hot water here."

Without ceremony Karl pointed out that thus far, they had found the remains of an extraterrestrial, uncovered the second crystal skull, been kidnapped, shot at, locked up, chased, cooped up in a crate and were currently riding piggy-back on a truck in a UFO.

"If that's not hot water, then I don't know what is. I don't know about you chaps, but I am prepared to see this through to conclusion—whatever that may be."

Neville couldn't help but agree with him, and Tito, actually impressed that this little, irksome man had finally shown some backbone, also agreed. Belinda looked a tad nervous but as she pointed out that it was three to one, she also agreed.

Neville walked over to the entrance of the craft, peered around the doorframe and found what he thought he was looking for. He extended his right arm and touched a small, purple oval panel with his hand. The panel was gelatinous to the touch with very little resistance so that he had the distinct impression that he was touching jelly.

The same clunking noises were heard followed by more hissing and the door slid back into place, shutting out the noise of their transport but as the door finally shut, the seal was so perfect that he had some difficulty finding the seam....

The electric blue lights faded but the interior retained its twilight hue.

"What are you doing, Neville?" asked Belinda. Neville turned to her.

"We might as well travel in comfort for a while, and besides, we stand a greater chance of avoiding discovery if we are in here instead of outside on the trailer."

"Good point," she added.

The True Architects

After what seemed almost an age, the truck stopped. They only became aware of this because Karl could see from the front view port that the tarpaulin had ceased flapping violently and the vague suggestion of silhouettes could be seen moving around outside.

"Um, I don't want to alarm anyone but I think it's hiding time!" Belinda got up from where she had been sitting and crossed the floor to where Karl was peering out of a triangular aperture.

"Get down!" she cried as the tarpaulin was whipped off of the wedge.

Cautiously, Tito and Neville also crept over to where the other two were crouching, and as they did so, Belinda very slowly peered out from the large front view port. The sight that she beheld made her heart race. The trailer had finally halted at the entrance to one of the caves that Tito had spoken of.

"I do hope that I'm not inconveniencing you by summoning you

104

here, Mr. Deveraux!" hissed the tall hooded figure as Deveraux and Reichstein walked up to the entrance of the cave.

"If you'd a given me more time and men, Ah would've got the rest of the skulls and wouldn't have had to waste ma time fart-arsing about with Weston and his goons!" retorted Deveraux.

The hooded figure, without saying a word, raised a slender white hand, and Deveraux felt an uncontrollable urge to reach for his pistol—before he knew it, the cold steel barrel of the pistol was at his temple

"If you value that calorie-laden, cigar smoking existence of yours, you will kindly remember to hold your tongue in my presence," hissed the hooded figure.

Beads of perspiration were forming on Deveraux's forehead and he was shaking ever so slightly.

"Yes, sir, I apologize for ma insolence." The figure lowered his hand and Deveraux dropped the pistol to the ground and stood there, shaking violently.

"Do you have the girl?" hissed the hooded figure. Reichstein had already returned to the jeep and was ousting Madeline from the back seat with the aid of a pistol.

"Sir," started Deveraux, "Ah have the Cerebratome and the craft as you asked, but the girl took a little more hard work to acquire," he said in a shaky voice.

The hooded figure sighed. "Will another five million be satisfactory, Mr. Deveraux?" answered the hooded figure.

Marcus grinned so hard that Madeline thought his face would split. "Your generosity knows no bounds, sir!" he replied.

"Yes, yes" answered the figure. "See one of these men," said the figure waving a hand in the direction of the group of men in white coats. "They will ensure that get your money." Deveraux turned to walk away when he felt a chillingly cold hand grasp his shoulder with unnaturally strong force.

"Before you depart, please be so kind as to tell me the fate of Mr. Weston and his associates?" Deveraux gulped hard. His breathing quickened.

"What's wrong, Mr. Deveraux? You don't look well. You didn't kill them did you?" said the figure, its voice taking on an evil sharpness.

"No!" cried Deveraux.

"No, sir, they…they…evaded us at the complex. Ah searched for them, really Ah did, but I had a call from there not an hour ago sayin' it was all clear. They musta got clean away out onto the plateau." The grip on Deveraux's shoulder tightened a little, making him wince then it released.

"No matter, you have done your job…for now. I will call for you later." The figure lifted its hand from his shoulder and raised it a little. A guard approached and the figure instructed him to dispatch a squad of helicopters to scour the plateau.

"I think that Mr. Reichstein can the handle the reins from here." Reichstein had returned with Madeline and she was thrust into the arms of two waiting guards.

"Yes, mien heir," he replied in his weaselly voice.

With that said and done, the convoy was started again and the vehicles proceeded to enter the cave past the guards, Madeline, Deveraux and the tall hooded figure. Belinda remarked to herself just how tall this figure was. It was abnormally tall for any human. While she was thinking, Neville crawled over to her.

"Now might be a good time to plan an emergency egress from this craft," he said. Belinda agreed and as she nodded, they noticed a sudden drop in the light outside.

"We must be in a tunnel," remarked Karl.

"Now I think is the time," said Tito and with that, Neville got up and quickly darted over to the door and depressed the jelly-panel. The door slid open and they noticed that it was getting lighter up ahead. Neville cautiously looked out of the door behind them to see if there were any vehicles following them, but, as luck would have it, they were last in the convoy and it was clear that had to make a jump for it. The truck was only rolling along at about ten miles an hour so there wasn't any serious danger of major injury, except if they collided with the tunnel wall. Without hesitation, Neville dropped from the craft and threw himself from the trailer and landed on the soft soil that lined the tunnel. Belinda followed and Tito was about to jump but he felt a tug at his shirtsleeve. Karl had a look of sheer terror in his eyes

"I can't do it!" he exclaimed, but Tito was not in the mood for childish fears.

"Okay! You staya here and take your chances with all those men and their guns!" Karl's eyes widened even further, and as Tito jumped, he felt a pair of chubby arms grip him around the waist and they both tumbled from the craft onto the soft soil with Tito landing first and Karl collapsing on top of him. Belinda and Neville came running up out of the gloom.

"It's okay! I'm fine," exclaimed Karl as he sat up but Tito was face down in the dirt cursing to himself.

With an air of certain urgency, Neville ousted Tito from his rambling and helped him up. Belinda and Karl were already making their way across the tunnel to the shadows on the opposite side. Tito and Neville soon joined them. Karl was trying hard to avoid eye contact with Tito.

"What now?" he exclaimed.

"Now, we enter the belly of the beast once more!" replied Neville with a decidedly theatrical tone.

In single file, they crept along the tunnel wall as quickly as they could until they could see around the bend. In what was probably the largest cavern any of them had seen was the most bizarre menagerie of military style equipment, vehicles, weird fluid-filled structures and numerous isolation tanks dotted around the floodlit floor, and near to where the entrance opened out into the cavern was a disused mobile generator of immense dimensions and it was this, much like the crates in the mountain complex, that would serve as a covered position from which they could observe without being seen.

One by one, on each other's signal, they darted across the shadowy corner of the cavern to the generator. Karl, being Karl, stumbled, fell over and very nearly ended up being seen by a sentry posted not ten yards away.

Once they were ensconced behind the generator, Belinda crawled beneath the generator and took up a position behind the foremost wheel arches. Tito mimicked her at the other end of the vehicle with Neville and Karl perched in the grubby, dirt-encrusted cab.

Neville carefully wiped a small area from one of the windows so that he could peer out without being observed, but as soon as he had taken up a position of observation, he felt a tug at his arm. He turned to a scowling face and silent lips. Karl was glowering at him and Neville huffed, rolled his eyes and rubbed a second patch of window clear for Karl to peer out of as well.

After a short period, Tito began to fidget. He couldn't get comfortable, as having the hefty bulk of Karl Weston landing on top of him had put a considerable strain on his poor back. Belinda hissed to get his attention and motioned for him to be quiet as she pointed out to the center of the cavern floor. In the distance amidst the thrum of the machinery and works, a tall burly man roughly the same shape and size of Deveraux was walking next to a tall hooded figure. The burly man was clad in military fatigues and had the most outrageously large black moustache, which made him look more like a circus ring master than anything else.

The two figures stopped some yards from where Belinda and the others were hidden, and Belinda could see that they were deep in conversation with the mustached man, bowing almost in reverence from time to time. What were they saying and who was this mysterious hooded figure? Belinda was rolling the idea of the identity of this strange figure through her mind, when the hooded figure outstretched one, then both arms and patted the burly man on the shoulders in a sympathetic gesture and then came the shock that none of them had expected. From beneath the folds of cloth that made the hood and cloak concealing this stranger, two more arms appeared and they pulled back the hood to reveal the stranger's face.

Belinda gasped as she suddenly made a quick mental leap from the skeleton on the plateau to the skulls to this creature before her. She felt her pulse racing, and she had broken out in a cold sweat. She could see the marked resemblance of the skeleton unearthed up on the plateau to this living, breathing facsimile. The figure's head was devoid of hair but one major similar feature was the broad, flat forehead and the defining jaw that gave the head a distinctly square, no, oblong appearance. The creature's skin was milky white with faint, marbled patches of blue here and there. Its eyes were rather small in comparison, but it did have a large broad nose, and Belinda, seeing the skull fleshed out, suddenly realized where she had seen this likeness before. "The stone heads of Easter Island," she silently mouthed to herself.

She looked over at Tito who was there, mouth open and staring in blank astonishment. In the cabin, Karl had recoiled in terror from the slit but Neville was glued to the scene.

"A real extraterrestrial!" he said over and over.

The figure pulled its hood back over its head and retracted the second pair of arms before turning from the burly man and walking back the way they had come. The burly man mopped his brow and fingered his collar nervously before hurrying towards the tunnel entrance.

Belinda shook herself from her torpor and realized that there was an urgent need for action. She quietly crawled over to Tito, who was still led in the same position, his eyes fixed on the point where the two figures had been standing.

"Tito," whispered Belinda. No answer.

"Tito," she whispered louder and shook him by the shoulder. His pallid face turned to her and she could see that he was frightened.

"Come on, we'd better check on Karl and Neville," she whispered.

While Belinda and Tito crawled from under the vehicle, Neville was still transfixed at the window. He was so engrossed in watching the tall figure disappear into the darkness on the far side of the cavern that he failed to notice that Karl was whimpering in hysterics and cowering in the foot well of the cab.

Tito and Belinda were now behind the cab and Belinda rattled at the door handle, the sound of which made Karl cry out inarticulately.

"Sssshhh, they'll hear you!" hissed Neville, not taking his eyes from the window. Suddenly the door catch popped and Belinda quickly stepped back and pulled the door open. Karl was ready for any alien assailants that might want to suck out his brains or probe him in unpleasant places, and as the door opened fully, he put all his weight into his legs and booted the first thing he saw, which unfortunately happened to be the peering face of Tito.

Karl's feet connected with Tito's face with a sickening crunch, and Tito recoiled in pain as he stumbled and fell against the cavern wall some feet behind him.

"Jesus, Karl!" hissed Belinda, but Karl was too shocked to take stock of what he had just done.

By this time, Neville was roused from his peepshow by the commotion behind him and was desperately trying to calm Karl down whilst Belinda helped Tito stem the flow of crimson blood that was streaming from his nose.

"One of these days, Belinda!" said Tito in a stuffy voice.

The burly mustached man had made his way to the tunnel mouth and was talking into the radio that he had plucked from his belt. Belinda left Tito pinching his nose and soaking up the excess blood with the other torn sleeve from her dirty shirt. She very cautiously made her way to the back of the generator truck and peered around the rear bumper. Less than fifteen feet away stood the burly man with his back to her. He was very broad shouldered and she could see that like Deveraux he evidently had a fondness for food. He had a shock of black hair, graying at the sides, which had been cut into a sharp military flattop, but the most poignant feature was that huge moustache that adorned his bulldog-like face. She could see that he was talking into a radio, his voice seemed muffled but she distinctly heard the names "Deveraux" and "Pullman" mentioned in this conversation.

She was about to return to the others when she heard one word clear as day, that word was *eliminated.*

Did this man intend for Deveraux to dispose of Madeline or did it mean that were both to be eliminated? She couldn't tell, but this was getting really serious and she was beginning to think that Karl was right. Had they gotten in too deep? What was the creature they had just witnessed talking to this new and formidable man? Why was there no indication of a major government involvement, and if Deveraux was but a pawn in this whole affair, who was at the top overseeing the actions of countless others? And the most important question that burned foremost in her mind, what did whoever was at the top want with the skulls?

Later, after Neville, Belinda and Tito had succeeded in calming Karl down in the safety of the shadows behind the generator truck (Tito's attempt at calming Karl down by punching him repeatedly in the face was thwarted by Belinda), they started planning what to do next.

"Now we're here, how do we move from this spot? We have absolutely no cover beyond this truck," remarked Karl, his voice still trembling slightly.

Neville frowned as he remarked that Karl was right. "It would appear that we are in something of a rut here. What's our next move?"

Belinda, for the first time since this whole affair began out on the remote plateau, felt totally and utterly helpless and she could sense that the others shared a similar feeling.

A shadowy figure ascended a narrow staircase and entered a chamber that was dimly lit by a diffused electric blue light and light breeze wafted up the exposed stairwell, causing the figure's robes to flutter slightly.

"Our plan is nearing completion," whispered the tall, shadowy figure.

From the gloomy corners of the chamber, two other figures similarly clad in drab hooded robes appeared.

"Has the human Deveraux found the last of the skulls?" hissed one of the three.

"There are still eight to be collected, but we are aware of the exact location of seven and they are being acquired as we speak," hissed the first tall figure.

Slowly all three figures made their way to the center of the chamber under the diffused light, and one by one, they pulled back their hoods. Their oblong, near featureless faces seemed almost human had it not been for the pallid complexion and the patchy blotches of blue on their skin.

One of the three had an abundance of blue patches adorning his face so that he had the markings similar to that of a piebald. This one was showing chronic signs of fatigue and physical stress.

"We must complete the plan quickly. Our time is running out." The first of the figures raised his hand. "Patience, brother. Soon, time will no longer matter."

The shortest of the three shot a cold stare to the first. "We are dying!" he retorted. "We must have the skulls in order to survive."

The first figure was about to speak when heavy footsteps were heard ascending the staircase to the chamber. "Brothers, depart. I will contact you again soon." And with that, the two pulled up their hoods again and almost floated back into the shadowy corners of the chamber while the first remained with his hood down, facing the entrance.

The big, mustached man entered and bowed in reverence.

"I do hope I am not intruding, sir," he said in a broad European accent.

The figure smiled thinly, the sort of smile that made you scared, not comfortable.

"Mr. Langstrom, what news do you bring me?" Ernst Langstrom was sweating heavily and in the blue light of the chamber, the beads of perspiration glistened as they cascaded down his face.

This man was showing signs of extreme nervousness.

"I bring word of the acquisition of five of the skulls, sir," he said in a shaky voice.

"Excellent news," replied the figure.

Langstrom remained for a few seconds, fidgeting nervously, and then he turned to leave.

"Was there something else Mr. Langstrom?" inquired the figure.

Ernst froze on the spot, his eyes wide facing away from the figure. "Um, well, there was one other thing, sir. The recon squad has found no trace of Mr. Weston and his associates anywhere on the plateau...sir." There was a pregnant pause, which to Ernst seemed to last an eternity.

"Well, that can only mean that they are here, can it not?" answered the figure.

Ernst felt the powerful grip of a cold hand on his shoulder; he shuddered at the touch.

"Find them, incapacitate them if need be, but bring them to me unharmed," was the reply.

Ernst turned to the figure. Its face was set like stone, showing no signs of emotion.

When Ernst had first seen this face nearly ten years ago, he felt very vulnerable and powerless back then and the same feeling asserted itself every time he was in their presence.

He nodded frantically and made a hasty exit out of the chamber and almost fell down the staircase as his body nearly overtook his feet in his hastened attempt to distance himself from these intimidating creatures.

After Ernst Langstrom had composed himself, he set about organizing several search parties to scour the cavern, but it had to be conducted in a very discreet manner.

Deveraux was sitting in a chair and leaning back on the rear legs, rocking gently with his feet on the table as he puffed on another of his foul-smelling cigars

"Ya know Reichstein, I guess working for these guys ain't so bad," he said as Reichstein entered the room in which he was sat. "At least they pay well!" he chuckled.

Reichstein sneered at him. "Is money all you think of? You Americans can be so nearsighted sometimes." Deveraux stopped rocking back on the chair and fixed his eyes on Reichstein as he crossed the room to a large cupboard that stood on the far wall.

"What the hell are you in it for then?" Deveraux quizzed.

Reichstein spun around and slammed his clenched fists on the table "Power!" he almost shouted through gritted teeth. "Nearly half a century ago, my fatherland almost conquered the free world, and now I have an opportunity to dominate the entire globe!"

Deveraux played with the cigar between his yellow teeth for a few moments. "You got the wrong idea about these here visitors." He indicated the word *visitors* in inverted commas with his fingers. "All they want is the skulls and that other doohickey, and then they're gonna skid addle outta here! After all, it was them that dropped 'em here all those years ago and we just been keepin' 'em safe till they came and got 'em."

Reichstein's expression changed. He stood up and started to laugh manically.

"You fat stupid fool! You really don't understand what's happening here, do you!"

Deveraux shot from his chair and quick as lightning had Reichstein pinned to one wall by the throat. "What in the name o' Sam Hill are you talkin' 'bout?" He was wringing Reichstein's neck like a Christmas turkey.

"Spit it out before I beat it outta you!"

Reichstein started turning blue and was putting up no resistance whatsoever, which made Deveraux realize that this was not the way to extract information from a cool customer like this.

He was about to let him down when the door opened and in walked Ernst Langstrom, who, seeing what was happening, instantly gripped Deveraux's arm and tried to pull it from Reichstein's neck. Deveraux released his grip, and Reichstein slumped to the floor and took in great gulps of air.

Ernst turned to Marcus. "What do you think you are doing? Are you mad?" Deveraux straightened his top and sat back down in the chair.

"I wanna know what's goin' on and I wanna know now!" he demanded.

Ernst sighed. "Wilhelm, leave us and help look for those idiots Weston and Whitt!"

Reichstein got up and skulked from the room, but as he left, he glared at Deveraux with incalculable malice, Deveraux just smiled. "Shut the door on the way out! There's a good boy!" Ernst sat on the corner of the table and toyed with one end of his oversized moustache "We must stick together on this, Marcus. Remember, they are the enemy, not the likes of Reichstein."

Deveraux still didn't trust Ernst Langstrom any more than he trusted Wilhelm Reichstein, but he certainly liked Langstrom better.

"Here's what they are planning to do..." began Ernst.

Chapter 16

An Uneasy Agreement

"We've sat here for nearly two whole hours!" moaned Karl.

Neville was getting rather uncomfortable as well. "I must admit, I'm frightfully thirsty and also a tad hungry. It must be nearly twenty four hours since we last ate."

Belinda was also beginning to feel the physical strain of this endeavor. She looked over at Tito who was looking rather worse for wear. He thus far had sustained a beating from Deveraux's goons, had a reel of cable dropped on his head, been punched, kicked, flattened and thumped, and all except the incident with Deveraux's men seemed to have been administered by the fat little sweaty man that sat next to him drawing pictures in the loose earth with his finger.

Belinda noticed that Tito still had the remnants of dried blood around the base of his nostrils. Karl too was a shadow of his former self—dirty, sweaty and sporting a rather fine black eye courtesy of Tito.

"We have to get water from somewhere," she added.

Karl slowly got to his feet, accidentally flicking dirt into Tito's face in the process. "I don't know about acquiring water, I certainly need to dispense some!" And he waddled penguin-fashion to the end of the truck nearest the cave mouth.

At this point, Neville started mouthing a word and pointing at the tunnel mouth, Belinda saw what he was indicating and a cold shiver ran down her spine. Not thirty feet from where they were hidden, a single, solitary guard was marching towards their position, and if he walked a foot or so to the left, he'd see Karl relieving himself, and that's exactly what happened.

The others had dived beneath the truck to remain unobserved, and Belinda and Neville were whispering hoarsely at Karl to get his attention but the splashing sound of excess water hitting the cavern floor was mingling with their hissing voices and he failed to hear them.

Karl was quietly whistling to himself as the shadow rose over him and darkened his corner.

"Do you mind, can't a gentleman relieve himself in private any—"

He didn't get to finish the sentence because he felt the barrel of a rifle shoved into the small of his back.

"Excuse me, but I think you shoes are untied." The guard was baffled at the second voice and turned to face a thin wiry man with wispy white hair and a pair of bent steel rim glasses perched on the end of his nose.

Quick as a flash, Neville had snatched the rifle from the surprised guard's hands, and from beneath the truck, a muscular pair of arms emerged and gripped the ankles of the guard before pulling his feet out from under him.

The guard hit the floor with a thud and was dragged under the truck where a stifled cry was silenced by the satisfying smack of fist on flesh. What didn't sound too good was the harsh feminine voice that followed, cursing at the pain and Belinda emerged from beneath the truck shaking her hand and wincing.

"Good god, Belinda!" remarked Karl. "Are you all right?"

Belinda ushered them back behind the tuck before staring at Karl, and managing a little grin, she said, "Um, Karl…"

She pointed at his crotch with her good hand. Karl saw Tito and Neville smirking and then realized that his fly was still open.

"Oh dear lord, how embarrassing!" he exclaimed as he turned away to do up his zipper.

Tito bent down and dragged the unconscious form of the guard from beneath the truck.

Neville stared "Look, he's nothing but a boy!"

The guard could not have been more than twenty years of age, but he was quite tall and rather stocky in build and he appeared to be of Latin American origin. Belinda looked at the guard and then at Tito, and Tito knew exactly what she was thinking. After some minutes of struggling to undress the guard, Neville had pulled a length of insulated wire from the generator truck's inner workings and this served as a makeshift rope with which to bind their insensible prisoner.

Moments later, Tito emerged dressed in the drab black and blue uniform complete with SWAT-style cap that bore the blazing emblem of a mighty fiery serpent bird.

"Looks more like a Phoenix to me," remarked Karl. Tito walked up to Karl and gripped one of his sleeves, smiled and then wrenched it from the rest of the jacket with a ripping sound.

"What the blue blazes…" Tito shot him a glare that silenced him immediately.

"Use-a this to gag him," he added as he handed the sleeve to Neville who's was tying the last of the bonds.

Belinda looked at Tito and he could see a tear forming in the corner of her left eye. She hugged him. "Please be careful! I don't want to lose you over some water and a scrap of bread."

Tito hugged her tight.

"Don't worry, Belinda, I'll be fine!" Neville and Karl turned their backs on this tender moment.

Belinda stood back with a tear in her eye, but then she stared at Tito's shirt.

"What's that?" she asked him, pointing at the strange pendant that had gotten snagged on one of the buttons of his shirt. Tito looked down at it and plucked it from the button.

"This was given to me by my father when I was a boy. It has been in our family for generations," he said as he gently fingered the pendant.

Belinda didn't recognize the mineral it was made from, but what did catch her attention was the bizarre shape it was carved into. It was an oddly angular crescent moon shape with four bars radiating from its center. He tucked it back into his shirt and laid a heavy hand on Karl's shoulder. He turned to see Tito smiling down at him.

"Take care while I'm gone, okay!"

Karl grinned back at him. "Will do, mon capitan!" he gleefully replied.

Neville shook him by the hand and wished him well as he handed him the rifle. "Don't be a hero now, okay?" And with that, Tito skirted from the shadows and darted into the tunnel mouth and emerged walking in a very military manner indeed.

"Do you think he'll pull it off, Belinda?" asked Neville with some reservation in his voice.

Belinda was frowning but she had no intention of making any off them feel any more stressed that they already were. "He'll be fine," she said, but inside she was worried sick.

"So, you see, we must stick together," said Ernst.

Deveraux was mulling something private over in his mind. "What I don't understand is why us?" If all they want is the skulls, why do they need our help?" Deveraux finally answered.

Ernst Langstrom got up from the table and walked over to the cupboard on the far end of the wall and pulled out a big wad of papers. He dropped them on the table in front of Deveraux and pointed to the top sheet.

"Read this," he said.

Deveraux scanned the paper with his eyes flicking across the text indicating that he was only surface reading.

"Ah don't care if they're from Scotland, just as long as they pay up."

Ernst sighed heavily. "There is more to life than money, Marcus. The reason they need our help is because they are dying and they have been dying ever since they first arrived eight thousand years ago. A small group was left behind to search for the skulls and keep their existence a secret from the then quite primitive inhabitants of Earth."

Ernst flicked through a few pages and stopped at a page of pictures, one of which was of the dirt-encrusted skeleton that had been dug up on the plateau by Belinda and her team.

"You see, Marcus, originally, there were twenty of them but they found it difficult to live in our atmosphere so they constructed the catacombs beneath this mountain range to sustain themselves."

Marcus Deveraux seemed totally unfazed by this news and just continued rolling the remnants of his cigar through his teeth. "So, they want the skulls and they had some secret organization, your organization build that thing for 'em using their technology so they could go home again?"

Ernst look a little relieved that he was finally making headway with the Texan.

"What's the whole affair with these skulls anyway?" asked Deveraux.

Tito was making his way over to the far side of the cavern in his search for provisions when he caught sight of the large organic looking structures that clustered in the middle of the cavern. They looked like opaque, fleshy termite mounds that had a viscous blue liquid bubbling inside them, and they were giving off a faint electric blue glow.

He didn't realize that he was staring, open jawed until a guard called in an irritated voice to him.

Tito spun around to see the man approaching at full speed.

"You there, what do you think you're doing! Got nothing to do, I see?" Tito was about to speak when the man, who judging by his heavily adorned uniform was obviously of senior rank, thrust a big black folder into his free hand while he was limply clutching the rifle in the other.

"Take this to Mr. Langstrom, cabin eighteen."

Tito looked at the folder and then looked at the man in front of him.

"What's the matter, forgotten your own bloody name?" said the man as he slapped Tito around the back of the head. The man was getting red in the face.

"Over there!" he shouted and he pointed with one stubby finger where he was supposed to be heading. "And for Christ's sake! Sort that uniform out!"

Tito was ready to lash out and floor the man, but then he remembered his position and made a few apologetic grumbles before lowering his head and heading off in the direction indicated.

Belinda and Karl gave a sigh of relief as they saw Tito walk away from the chief guard, for they had been watching his movements from the safety of the truck.

"Jesus that was close!" remarked Belinda. Neville was behind them, sitting cross legged on the floor evidently deep in thought.

Tito Headed over to the row of porta-cabins that had been set up along the rear wall of the cavern and he could see that there were great big black numbers on the side of them that made it easy for him to find eighteen.

He reached it soon enough, but he couldn't help but keep glancing over his shoulder at those weird fleshy liquid kopjes in the middle of the floor.

He finally paid attention to the task at hand and was about to knock on the door when he heard voices from inside. He waited a few moments, composed himself and rapped sharply on the door. The voices inside fell silent for a moment or two and then a gruff European voice shouted, "Enter!"

Tito turned the door handle and walked smartly into the room and got his first close up of the mustached man they had seen earlier.

"What is it?" said Ernst Langstrom, rather irritated by this untimely interruption. Tito said nothing and just shoved the black folder out in front of him "Ah, I've been waiting for this."

As Langstrom walked over to him, Tito saw the man that was sat in the chair behind Langstrom. Tito's eyes widened as he stared into the fat, repugnant face of Marcus Deveraux. Deveraux apparently hadn't held any interest in the guard until Langstrom asked where Captain Fiorna was, but Tito didn't answer for he nether knew where or who Captain Fiorna was.

"What's the matter, cat got your tongue? Speak, man!"

At this point Deveraux took notice and he nearly fell off of his chair when he saw who it was dressed as a guard before him. "YOU!" he shouted as he stumbled to his feet and rapidly drew his pistol from the unseen holster under his jacket.

Tito leveled the rifle towards Deveraux, but before ho could do anything, the startled Langstrom unintentionally dropped the heavy folder on the barrel of the gun and the rifle fell from Tito's hand and clattered on the floor of the cabin.

"At last!" scowled Deveraux. "Where in the name o' Henry have you been a'hidin'?"

Ernst looked a little bemused. "This is one of the Weston party, yes?"

Deveraux was grinning from ear to ear and darting glances towards Ernst as he covered Tito with his pistol.

"Oh yeah, this is that big ol' tough guy I had to deal with back at base one. Okay, buddy, where's the rest o' your friends hidin' at, huh?" snarled Deveraux.

Tito was so enraged; he just swore at Deveraux in English instead of Mexican and spat on the floor at his feet

"You'll gonna tell me or I'm gonna put a bullet in that head o' yours right now!" spat Deveraux.

"No!" cried Ernst. "The architects want them all alive!"

Deveraux's face took on the expression of a sulking child. "What the hell for?" he whined.

Slowly, one of the architects descended the stairs and entered the cavern. The multitude of men who were busy around the machinery moved to one side almost immediately upon seeing him arrive.

He headed for the fluidic domes in the middle of the floor and touched a nodule that protruded from a dark blue patch on the side of one conical structure. An opening, as if by magic, appeared and he disrobed and stepped through into the liquid mass, but none spilled out as the aperture closed behind him.

Within the dome, his outline was partially visible as he apparently engaged in some complex task involving the flailing of all six limbs in a rather sporadic fashion.

"Right!" snarled Deveraux as he sat Tito down in the chair at gunpoint. "Ah don't give a rat's ass about what them ganglions say! If you don't tell me where they are, I'm gonna instruct the guards to shoot on sight. Not to kill, but some o' them ain't the best shot in the world. Get me?"

Tito knew he was in a no-win situation and for all concerned, if they were taken prisoner again, this time under the apparently more level headed and humane duress of Langstrom, they may get the water and food they craved so much.

"They're behind the truck at the entrance to the tunnel!" he finally said.

"I do hope he's all right," said Karl as they crouched behind the truck.

"You will find out soon enough," said a voice behind them. They slowly turned to see three guards standing behind them with rifles trained on them.

"Oh crap!" said Karl.

Half an hour later, all four of them were reunited once more in the cabin, gagged and tied to chairs.

Deveraux and Langstrom were talking in hushed voices in the corner when the door burst open and in walked Reichstein with Madeline, her hands tied and a handkerchief stuffed into her mouth.

He shoved her to the side of the room where the others were seated and she almost collapsed on top of Neville.

"Isn't this nice!" whined Reichstein as he crossed the room to join Deveraux and Langstrom

Madeline succeeded in spitting out the handkerchief. She and Neville stared at each other for a few moments and then Madeline managed to loosen Neville's gag with her teeth.

"Oh, Neville, are you alright?"

Neville nodded. "I'm fine, my dear," he said in a partially muffled voice. "Where have you been?"

Reichstein passed some snide comment and made a wild gesture with his hands before Deveraux told him to "Shut your god damn mouth!" before the three of them stepped outside the cabin, locking the door behind them.

"Madeline, what on god's green earth is going on?" asked Neville in a concerned tone.

Madeline made her way along the line and in turn, using her teeth. she pulled down each of their gags one by one, after which she slumped to the floor in front of them.

"What do they want with you, Miss Pullman?" inquired Karl.

Madeline shifted awkwardly. "My father Tobias worked with Deveraux a few years ago and he disappeared whilst on an expedition to recover the jade parrot statue from Angkor Wot in Cambodia."

Belinda looked a little surprised. "I read about that; out of a party of seventeen, only eight were rescued when the caverns beneath the temple collapsed!"

Madeline nodded in confirmation of this. "Deveraux was one of the survivors, and one of the rescue team said that my father had been saved as well, but when I confronted Deveraux about it, he said that they must have been mistaken."

Karl was looking very angry at this point but said nothing.

"Eighteen months ago, I received a telephone call from a man claiming to be a friend of my father's and that he had been found in Bogotá alive and well. So I, thinking no more of it, came straight away and walked right into the clutches of Deveraux and Langstrom."

Karl couldn't hold his tongue any longer, "I swear, when this is over I will make Deveraux pay for this!"

Madeline looked at Karl and smiled thinly at him. "I later discovered that it was Langstrom who made the call ,and they told me that they knew the whereabouts of my father, but if I didn't help them on this project they where planning, I would never see him, not even his body if they killed him, which Deveraux threatened to do!"

Neville fidgeted, trying to loosen his bonds.

"Do you have any proof that they have your father?" asked Belinda.

Madeline looked up at her with watery eyes. "I don't know for sure but I can't take the risk of calling their bluff just in case," her voice was trembling slightly.

"What exactly do they want you to do for them?" asked Neville, still jostling with the ties that bound him to the chair.

"As Neville already knows, apart from astronomy I specialize in rare and ancient dialects."

Neville hummed his acknowledgment of this as he looked down behind him to check his progress.

"They told me that I had to decipher the markings on the Cerebratome and tell them what will happen when all thirteen skulls are assembled within it, but I can't! It's in an ancient root dialect that I have never seen before!" She held back a tear as she squirmed like Neville to loosen her bonds.

Suddenly the door burst open and in walked Deveraux, Langstrom and Reichstein.

"Looks our little jailbirds have been a yakking!" said Deveraux.

"Marcus, take Miss Pullman down to the Cerebratome," ordered Langstrom "We must have something. The architects are getting impatient."

Deveraux acknowledged this and lifted Madeline from the floor, and with the help of Reichstein, escorted her struggling form from the room.

Langstrom strode over and stood in front of them. "Why do you insist in making life so difficult for yourselves?" he said in an

R.J. FLUX

unusually compassionate manner.

Tito started hurling abuse at him but Belinda interceded.

"Mr. Langstrom, what are those creatures we saw earlier?" she asked in the most innocent manner possible.

"Miss Osborne, I haven't had a chance to meet you properly. I must admire your gusto over this whole affair. You have been very brave and given Mr. Deveraux a run for his money!" He chuckled quietly as he said this. "But I must insist that you halt any efforts to interfere with our plans from here on in."

Karl was almost growling as he was glaring at Langstrom.

"Mr. Whitt, it is quite possible that you may be able to help us."

Neville seemed insulted at the very idea. "You treat us like common criminals, threaten us, intimidate us and then you expect our cooperation?"

Belinda felt pleased with Neville after this very astute comment.

"Mr. Whitt, you and I both know that it is not every day one gets the opportunity to come face to face with a real, living extraterrestrial, and given your profession, I thought that you might be persuaded?" Neville didn't answer straight away.

"Neville!" squeaked Karl.

"Yes, I will help you, Mr. Langstrom. Only if my friends are allowed to leave of their own accord without any hindrances."

Karl gave a frustrated sigh and Tito just rolled his eyes.

"Now you know I can't honor that, Mr. Whitt," said Langstrom jovially, "but I can see to it that they are more comfortably accommodated and given a little more free rein."

Tito was beginning to see red.

"We are prisoners then?" retorted Neville.

"It is your own doing I'm afraid. If you hadn't pursued us this far, none of you would be sitting here, now" replied Langstrom..

Belinda sat bolt upright, her eyes aflame. "Screw you!" she almost screamed. "If that bastard Deveraux hadn't killed Perez, kidnapped me and tried to kill Neville in the first place, none of us would be here now!"

Langstrom, unperturbed by Belinda's outburst, clasped his chin with his hand and began pacing the room.

"Actually it was Wilhelm who murdered your friend, but I must stress that is was under no orders from me or Mr. Deveraux."

He continued to pace the floor, rubbing his chin as he did so.

"Okay, I will make you a deal, you help us and I promise on my life that when the project is completed, you will be allowed to leave of your own accord but not before."

Karl stamped his foot. "We will NEVER agree to those terms!" he shouted.

"Karl, it our best option!" said Belinda angrily.

"Very well, I will help you," said Neville, "but first, we need food and water."

Langstrom looked down at him, and Neville could see that unlike Deveraux this was a man with compassion.

"Your bargaining posture is highly dubious, Mr. Whitt, but what good is a mind if it is starved, eh?"

Langstrom was about to leave when Karl piped up. "Hang on, what's to stop us talking about all this WHEN you let us go, hey?"

Langstrom just smirked. "It's simple, my dear Mr. Weston, no one on this earth would ever believe you!"

And without another word, he left the cabin and locked to door behind him.

An hour or so later, they were in a sparse yet comfortable room, locked of course, but it was considerably larger and had a chiller, which contained bottled water and several boxes of military ration-style meals.

On the far wall were two sets of bunks, each having a fresh set of fatigues similar to Langstrom's laid at the foot of the mattress.

"Hardly the Ritz at Piccadilly, is it!" remarked Karl as he pulled the shirt over his head. He turned to see three faces, set with angry expressions glaring at him, and he knew that he'd said enough.

Chapter 17
The Demise of Wilhelm Reichstein

Down in another chamber beneath the cavern, Madeline was busily working her way around the Cerebratome and jotting down copies of the strange markings that adorned it.

"Well, are you any closer to deciphering the markings on this thing?" The weaselly voice of Reichstein was heard at the entrance of the chamber.

He slowly made his way into the chamber and walked around it, casting the occasional sneer at Madeline.

"I do hope that you don't dally; it will not do you or your father any good if you fail!"

Madeline could see that he was reveling in tormenting her with threats to her missing father.

"Haven't you got some boots to lick somewhere?" she replied.

Reichstein continued to circle the Cerebratome. "Oh, still trying to score points against me, how very scientific of you."

Madeline put down the Dictaphone and jotter and turned to him, resting her hands on the edge of the Cerebratome. "You really are the most pathetic excuse for a man I have ever had the displeasure of meeting."

She fixed her eyes on him as he continued to pace the floor. "Does your boss know that you're down here, hindering my work?"

Reichstein stopped pacing and looked at her quizzically. "Boss?" he asked her. "I have no boss. No one has autonomy over me."

He took a step closer towards her. His pale, watery gray eyes seemed totally devoid of any emotion or compassion as he stared at her. "I am my own maker and I intend to have the power that is so rightfully mine!" he said, now mere inches from her face.

"Ah don't remember giving you authorization to interrogate Miss Pullman!" said a gruff Texan voice from behind them.

Madeline never thought that she'd be glad to see Deveraux, but in this instance, she was.

"Get the hell outta here, will ya!" Reichstein grinned at Madeline before he departed.

"Be a pip and get Langstrom to send Neville Whitt down here!" said Deveraux as Wilhelm skulked past him out of the chamber. "Ah do apologize for that untimely intrusion, my dear."

Deveraux smiled a wry smile as he approached.

"How's the research coming? Ah don't know if you overheard that little comment earlier, but Mr. Whitt will be joining you soon."

Madeline was highly suspicious of Deveraux. He was the most odious man and caution was strongly advised. "Why is Neville being sent here? I can cope!" she snapped.

"Ma employers are becoming a little impatient. They need this doohickey working, ASAP." He smiled a little more, revealing his tobacco stained teeth. "You'll see—the sooner you do that, the sooner you can go and I can get paid!"

He was about to leave when she grabbed his sleeve. "Mr. Deveraux, what about my father?" she asked.

Marcus looked down at his arm, then at her. And she let go.

"You'll see daddykins soon enough!" he said, chuckling lightly as he departed, leaving her standing there looking quite distraught.

Reichstein was making his way across the cavern to the row of porta-cabins that lined the far wall when he was intercepted by Langstrom.

"Reichstein!" called Langstrom. "I've been looking for you. The last party is due to return soon and they have the twelfth skull with them. See to it that they are secured with the others." Reichstein nodded.

"Yes, sir," he said sarcastically. "By the way, sir, Mr. Deveraux has requested that Whitt join Pullman at the Cerebratome."

Langstrom, completely oblivious to the intentions of this vicious, power-hungry, little man, thanked him for the message and went to get Neville from the cabin. As he approached, he failed to see Reichstein hurriedly chatting to a small group of scientists and guards amongst the myriad of machines that encircled the liquid mounds in the center of the cavern.

"Stewed apples, I hate stewed apples!" complained Karl.

Tito just looked at him with severe annoyance and threw a packet of dehydrated beef casserole at him so that it slapped his forehead and fell into his lap.

"Wha...oh, thanks, old bean!" he said as he took the packet and tore it open, sending dry powdery particles into the air.

"Karl, I think you're supposed to open that little pouch in the top and pour the water in there," said Neville as he popped another piece of dried fruit into his mouth.

Belinda was quietly sitting on her bunk and peering through the narrow, metal slats that barred the single small window at the end of the cabin

"Neville, what do you suppose they are?" she asked.

Neville stopped trying to save Karl's beef stew and put down the remnants of the foil container as he rose from the floor.

"What are what?" he inquired.

"Those," said Belinda, pointing to the liquid filled kopjes that bubbled in their fluid phosphorescence at the center of the cavern "You know, I have no idea!" he said.

As he and Belinda peered into the poorly lit area, the lock turned in the door and in walked Langstrom. "Mr. Whitt, time to honor our agreement," he said in a most gentlemanly fashion.

Neville turned to him. "What's to happen to my colleagues while I am away?" he inquired.

Langstrom locked the door behind him and pocketed the black plastic keycard.

"They are quite safe and will receive adequate provisions while you are indisposed", he said, looking rather flustered. "Can we please hurry this along; my employers are getting rather impatient," said Langstrom.

Neville bade Karl, Tito and Belinda an informal farewell and pocketed a few more packs of dried fruit and a bottle of water before departing with Langstrom and heading across the cavern.

"Mr. Langstrom, might I inquire as to what those fluidic structures over there are?" asked Neville as they past one large clear decontamination tank containing two men in contamination suits and the skeleton Belinda and Tito had discovered up on the plateau nearly a week ago. God! Had it really been nearly a week?

Up until now, Neville hadn't given any thought to how long they had been here.

"You don't know much about our visitors, do you?" replied Langstrom as they walked among the machinery.

Neville noticed that there were far fewer people about the cavern floor than there were earlier. "Am I to assume that they are true extraterrestrials?" Neville asked.

Langstrom looked down at him as they walked. "Hard as it may be to accept, yes they are. They have been here for nearly eight thousand years, and those cones you speak of are a kind of cellular regeneration chamber that has served to prolong their lives."

Langstrom was slightly concerned that Neville didn't seem more shocked at this. "You seem to be taking this in your stride, Mr. Whitt," he finally said.

"Oh, yes, well I don't think it's really sunk in yet."

They finally arrived at the entrance to an elevator shaft and Langstrom ushered Neville into the elevator car before joining him and closing the metal gates. After descending for a few minutes in absolute silence, the car stopped and they stepped out into a large floodlit room in the center of which sat the Cerebratome.

"It really is a puzzling structure isn't it," said Langstrom as they approached Madeline, who was busily recording notes into the Dictaphone and scrawling into her jotter.

"Hello, Madeline," said Neville as Langstrom stood over them like a prom escort.

"Neville, nice to see you," she said in a very flat tone.

"Well, I'll leave you to it," said Langstrom, smiling as he spoke.

"If you should need anything, tools and the like, there are two guards outside. One of them will see to it that you get what you need."

He patted both Madeline and Neville on a shoulder. "Time is of the essence now, I expect to some results by morning!" And with that he turned and left, leaving the two scientists looking quite at a loss as to what to say to each other.

"Damn this waiting around!" whined Karl as he sat peering from the window. "Hello, where's he off to?" he said.

This made Tito and Belinda approach the window as well.

"What is it, Karl?" asked Belinda. Karl pointed out from the window to a thin, hunched figure that was doing its best to avoid being seen as it approached the liquid-filled kopjes in the center of the cavern.

"That'sa Reichstein!" remarked Tito.

As they watched, they could see him skulking along behind some big units of machinery towards the cellular regenerators, and they noticed the heavy black haversack he carried in his hand.

"What the deuce is he up to over there?" Karl said to himself.

They all watched intently for some minutes, and Tito, being the tallest, could see past most of the obstructions and was straining to observe the actions of Wilhelm in the gathering gloom. One by one, the main spot lights were going out in sequence, leaving only the auxiliary lights casting a twilight glow over the vast floor of the cavern.

"So, Madeline, how are you doing…?" said Neville, placing one hand on the Cerebratome

"Actually, it might pay for us to put our past behind us for the moment and concentrate on this thing," she replied.

She began to show him the notes she had made and pointed out the top of the tier that had bizarre engravings on it.

"I'm sure it's a language," she said.

Around the circumference of the upper tier, just below the intricate gold workings that surmounted the Cerebratome were individual markings of lines and dashes.

"But take a look at these!" she pointed to the outer rim of the dais that ran just below the thirteen sockets.

Neville remarked at how much cleaner the object was since he had last seen it. "They could be numbers?" he said at last, but Madeline made plain that they were nothing like the text on the upper tier.

"What are you suggesting, Madeline?" said Neville as he bent down to make a closer inspection of the markings.

"I think its two different languages, and the most worrisome thing is I don't think our resident ETs have any real claim to it."

Neville gave her a puzzled look. "Go on," he said.

"Well, if they had been here for eight thousand years guarding this thing, how come they need our help to decipher it?"

Neville bent down and examined the lower set of symbols that ran the circumference. These were composed of tiny pictographs, each one having an increasing number of markings. He stood up and smiled at her. "Why did I ever let you get away?" he said.

Madeline smiled sheepishly at him and turned away. "Come on, we need to get this thing figured out before we tell them anything." And so the two set to work analyzing, reading and re-reading the symbols and pictographs that adorned the object as the light of the day outside grew dim and the plateau played host to a ceiling of dazzling white stars far above them.

Tito was snoring heavily on his bunk and Belinda was dozing on the one below him. Karl, still wide awake, sat transfixed at the window waiting to see if anything further happened.

His eyelids became heavy and he knew that he really ought to sleep. He hadn't slept properly for ages and the bunk did seem really inviting, but he resisted.

His observant vigil paid off about three hours later. The cavern floor was deserted with the exception of one or two sleepy looking guards here and there when he suddenly spotted the unmistakable outline of Reichstein slinking across to the regenerators again. What on earth could he be doing over there? Karl then spotted from the far corner near one of the stairwell entrances, three hooded figures proceeding towards the regenerators.

A cold shiver ran down his spine as he watched the shortest one disrobe, exposing that weird flat head, tapered body and four slender arms. This figure however, was nearly all blue with patches of white and it looked frail, very frail.

The two other hooded figures helped this third into the regenerator, and the fluid inside began to bubble and fizz. The phosphorescence produced by this effervescence illuminated a large portion of the cavern in a pale electric blue light. While this was happening, Karl saw Reichstein dart away from behind the regenerators and sprint into the darkness.

Karl fancied that he felt a slight trembling beneath his feet and his attention was once more drawn to the regenerator. It was bubbling violently and jerking in all directions, and he fancied that amidst the fizzing and bubbling he heard someone or something screaming.

Suddenly, there was a thunderous pop and the regenerator burst like an overfilled water balloon.

The two hooded figures immediately sought cover as the remains of the liquid spattered in all directions and illuminated parts of the cave with its phosphorescence where it hit.

Suddenly, all hell broke loose and there was a frenzy of excitement as people came streaming from porta-cabins; off-duty guards in nothing but their shorts came running to and fro in front of Karl's window.

The bang had roused Belinda from her slumber, but Tito continued snoring.

"What the hell was that?" called Belinda from her bunk.

"I think that one of our alien friends has departed in a most unpleasant fashion," said Karl coldly, not tearing his gaze from the window.

Outside, the commotion was dying down and Karl could now see Langstrom and Deveraux directing clean-up crews in contamination suits. Langstrom wore a flustered expression and looked almost frightened, while Deveraux just had the same agitated, rubicund face that he always had.

"God damn it, Ernst!" exclaimed Deveraux. "What in hell's gone on here? There's gonna be hell to pay for this and Ah ain't takin' the blame on this one!" he said as he surveyed the remains of the exploded regenerator. "They're gonna be mighty ticked off over this, Ah can tell ya!"

In the midst of the evaporating liquid, the mangled and distended remains of the third alien lay lifeless and still on the ground.

"You and you get this outta ma sight!" bellowed Deveraux to two passing guards. They both looked squeamishly at the slimy, glistening remains with its dead eyes staring up at them.

Karl and Belinda clapped their hands over their ears and Karl saw from the window that everyone else was doing the same. Their air had suddenly filled with a bloodcurdling, high pitched shriek. Deveraux fell to his knees, and Ernst was stumbling around madly, desperately trying to avoid the noise. Karl saw through squinting eyes a bright blue light emanating from the remains of the dead alien. The light spiraled upwards in a cumulus cloud before forming a glowing ball of crackling blue light that hung in the air above it. Slowly, the shrieking diminished by degrees until it had become a low level hum. Karl shook his head but he still had a violent ringing in his ears. He and Belinda watched as the ball of light slowly passed over Deveraux, Langstrom and the guards and floated over to a shadowy corner of the cavern. The two hooded figures followed it as it stopped above one of the porta-cabins, crackling wildly.

Ernst and Deveraux had also followed it.

Karl cursed under his breath as it passed out of his sight.

One of the hooded figures gestured for one of them to open the porta-cabin's door and Langstrom drew his pistol while Deveraux kicked the door in with his boot.

As the door swung open, the sound of a pistol round cracked, and Deveraux was hurled back and lay sprawled on the ground. He whimpered as he clutched his left knee. Crimson blood was gushing from the bullet wound. Langstrom jumped back from the doorway and cocked his pistol.

"Don't worry, Ernst; you are not in any danger. That was just a little payback for the ill treatment I received while under the command of this buffoon," hissed Reichstein from within the shadows of the dark cabin.

"Reichstein, you fool! What have you done?" bellowed Langstrom as he saw the two hooded figures floating away from the cabin.

One of them beckoned to Langstrom to do the same.

"Done? What have I done?" said Reichstein. "I have taken control of the situation, that is what I've done," he said in a disturbingly calm voice.

Deveraux was clawing his way away from the cabin as another shot ricocheted in the earth by his head. "Not so high and mighty now, are you!" called Reichstein from the shadows of the cabin as further shots embedded themselves in the ground around Deveraux. Langstrom leveled his pistol and fired a single round into the door of the cabin and they saw the dark shape dart from the doorway. In that instant, Langstrom rushed over and helped Deveraux onto his good leg and they hobbled as quickly as they could from the cabin. From the gloom of the cabin doorway, the pale face and sunken eyes of

Reichstein emerged, his lank hair hanging in greasy bangs across his low forehead. "You think that they will reward you for your servitude? You IDIOTS!" shouted Reichstein as he clutched the sides of the doorframe.

They now saw that the arm that held the gun was blistered and burnt with purple-blue patches, and he was sweating heavily. "They are the true enemy! They will destroy us all!"

He started to laugh insanely but his laughter died suddenly, and they saw mania give place to horror on his face as he looked up.

The humming blue orb was slowly descending through the ceiling into the cabin, and it suddenly caught him in its whipping electrical tendrils before encompassing him in crackling electricity.

He screamed with agony as the whips of blue lightning coursed through his body and lifted him into the air. He hung there for a minute or so, convulsing madly, and then suddenly there was a deafening crack and the blue light winked out in an instant, leaving the smoking body of Reichstein to slump the floor.

Deveraux and Langstrom looked on in half horror, half astonishment, but as they watched, the still smoking frame rose up on one arm then two, and the faintly glowing carcass of Wilhelm Reichstein unsteadily staggered onto its feet and slowly walked over to the two hooded figures that stood behind Langstrom and Marcus.

"This body will suffice for now," said a voice that certainly wasn't that of Wilhelm Reichstein.

Chapter 18
The Unlocking of the Cerebratome

Far beneath the main cavern, Madeline and Neville were totally oblivious to the explosive events that had passed above them.

"I just don't get it!" said Madeline, showing definite signs of frustration. "How long have we been at this now?" she asked.

"Nearly five hours," replied Neville as he consulted his small, silver battered pocket watch. "Time for a break, I think," he said.

Madeline gave a sigh of relief and they sat on the edge of the Cerebratome.

"Apple?" asked Neville as he offered the small foil bag of dried apple pieces to Madeline.

"Thanks," she replied.

She took a piece of apple and popped it into her mouth. As she chewed, she absentmindedly scanned the back of the bag reading the ingredients in various languages.

"That's IT!" cried Madeline. Neville jumped at the sudden outburst. "What's it, Madeline?" he said.

She slid off the edge of the Cerebratome and pointed to the panel on the back of the bag with the different languages on it. "Look!" she said "All languages have a root dialect, right?" Neville nodded as he slowly chewed on a piece of apple.

"If you take any base dialect, some of the letters or basic contributing phrases and change the root lettering, you can change the entire language. The Egyptians used pictograms and hieroglyphics as their writing, and this looks like it could be similar." Neville took another look at the markings. "Each one of these pictograms has a different combination of symbols." He pointed to the one closest to him. "Look at this one."

The pictogram was composed of a crescent moon shape with three lines emanating from its core, and the one preceding it had only two lines.

"Now look at the top tier," he said excitedly.

They both hunted around the dais until they found the symbol they were looking for.

"This can't be right," said Madeline.

"If it's meant to line up, then it's out of position by seven places and this thing is solid, no moving parts."

Neville scratched his head. "I think I have an idea."

Tito finally woke from his slumber, yawned, stretched and scratched himself in two places at once. "Whatsa so interesting?" he said as he saw Belinda and Karl glued to the window. No answer

"Hey!" he called out, and Karl answered him by glowering at him and making a *sssshhh* sound.

Tito got up and went to the chiller, got some water and began to guzzle it down thirstily.

"What did I miss?" he said in a hushed tone.

"Come here!" said Belinda, ushering him with one hand.

Tito stumbled to the window and peered out from between Karl and Belinda.

"Bloody 'ell!" he said as he surveyed the damage that had happened while he was sleeping. "Did war break out or some-a-thing?"

Belinda and Karl both relayed to him what they had seen, and he listened intently as he took it all in. "And that's when I saw this blue floating ball of light drift over there!" said Karl finally.

"Has there been any word from Neville yet?" he asked.

Belinda shook her head. "Nothing now for five hours," she said, looking at her watch.

"I hope he doesn't do anything stupid," said Karl as he rested his chin on his folded arms and continued to stare from the window.

"Ready?" asked Neville as he rested his head in one of the sockets that surrounded the Cerebratome.

"Is this really such a good idea?" asked Madeline.

Neville looked cockeyed at her from his doubled-over position "What is science?" he asked her. "The ability to take a risk, see the reaction, record the outcome and analyze the facts available to you in order to generate a plausible hypothesis," he said all in one breath.

"Oh, very text book, Neville!" she said as he took her position opposite him.

"On my mark....Mark!" said Neville as he forced his head into the socket as far as it would go. Simultaneously, Madeline tried to turn the dais in either direction, and she thought that for a second, it budged just a little.

Neville called to her and as she looked over, she could see a hunched back and a pair of arms waving aimlessly in the air.

After some minutes of struggling, Madeline managed to dislodge Neville's head from the socket "Right! I won't be trying that again!" he said as he tried to straighten his already wispy, messed up hair.

"If only we had one of the skulls to practice with!" said Madeline with a sigh.

"How about we do as Langstrom said and ask a guard to get one for us?" suggested Neville.

"I think you damaged a few gray cells when you got your head stuck," retorted Madeline. "I highly doubt it!" she added.

Neville went to the elevator and got into the car. "Won't be long!" he said in cheery tone, and she watched him ascend the shaft in the little metal cage.

Upon reaching the top, Neville swung open the gate and walked out onto a scene of utter chaos. Blue-purple luminous liquid was spattered in patches all over the cavern and there appeared to be a frenzy of activity over by one of the cabins.

Hmm, no guards, he thought to himself as he walked out onto the cavern floor. There were guards and men in white coats hurriedly darting from place to place, and over in one corner, there was an inexplicable electric blue haze, which seemed to be the major cause of all the excitement.

As he walked, he thought it strange that no one seemed to be paying him any attention, but he, on the rare occasion being quick off the mark, took the incentive to try and covet one of the skulls.

He skirted around the perimeter of the cavern and passed the generator truck behind which they had been hidden when they had first arrived.

Soon, Neville passed the cabin that the others were imprisoned in, but he was too busy thinking about how to obtain a skull to realize until he heard a frantic tapping on glass and turned to see the faces of Belinda, Tito and Karl peering through the slatted window of the cabin.

"Oh! Hello, chaps!" he said as he waved to them. Karl and Belinda were pointing behind them, indicating to the door. He realized how stupid it was to wave at them and rushed back to try the door, but it was still locked.

Neville ran back to the window. "Stay put; you're safe in there!" he said and headed off in the direction of the fluid regenerators.

"What in the world does he think he's doing?" said Karl as they watched him skitter off amid the machinery that littered the floor of the cavern.

"I don't know, but I know what he should be doing!" said Belinda as she stamped her foot hard on the floor.

As Neville walked amongst the contamination chambers and the spilt fluid, he noticed the rapidly decomposing remains of something organic.

Naturally being of a scientific mind, he went back to the nearest chamber, darted into the ante-room and grabbed a few screw-top test tubes that were lying on a cabinet top.

Neville returned to the mass of bubbling white, purple and blue liquid and scooped up a tube-full.

As he stood up, he saw through the window of the farthest examination chamber a glass skull case similar to the one shown to him and Karl by Deveraux in the first complex, and he headed straight for it.

Upon reaching it, he found the examination room empty, and to his great luck, the ruby skull sat in a cradle, clamped to the work top with a variety of tools laying on the bench beside to it.

Neville tried to remove the skull but it wouldn't budge so he tried to dislodge the clamp. No joy there either. Then he spotted a discarded fire axe and some other safety equipment that had obviously been disturbed from its cabinet when the frantic exodus from the room had occurred earlier.

Down in the chamber, Madeline stopped examining the Cerebratome when she heard the elevator motor start up. Moments later Neville emerged from the elevator car with the ruby skull, still attached to the examination frame, clamps and a jagged piece of dull gray Formica work top.

One of the guards had just finished bandaging Deveraux's leg when the tallest of the hooded figures came over to where he lay.

"The man Reichstein is no more. He has assassinated one of us and now he has paid the ultimate price." Deveraux was shaking with fear

"Ah knew nothin' of this, Ah swear!" he whimpered.

"We are aware of this, and we will take no further action." The figure raised one hand

"The Cerebratome must be operational within thirty six of your hours. If it is not, then you will share the same fate of Reichstein," it said in its steely calm voice.

Langstrom was stood only a few feet away and was trembling at the thought of being deleted and his body being used as a vessel for one of these cold, calculating creatures.

"It's no good, Karl, its locked!" said Belinda for the eighth time.

Karl was frantically attacking the lock with his pudgy hands and an empty water bottle.

"Give it up," said Tito as he jumped onto the top bunk. He lay back with his arms folded behind his head and sighed heavily.

"Damn it, damn it all to hell! I can't just sit here and wait while things are happening. I need to be in control!" whined Karl.

Belinda could see that Karl was beginning to exhibit the early signs of a nervous breakdown.

She too was feeling the strain of being imprisoned with no information about what was happening around her.

CRACK! Karl stopped attacking the lock with the bottle and Belinda also turned her attention to sound.

CRACK! The sound came again. Tito had noticed, as he lay back on the bunk, a seam in the ceiling that joined two of the panels together, and he was attempting to split them apart with a piece of bed frame he had managed to pull loose.

"Maybe we can get out through the roof!" he said as dust and pieces of ceiling were flying off the bunk and pinging onto the floor. With a dull thud, Tito realized with anger that the roof was made of the same sturdy metal as the door.

"Shit! We're going nowhere!" he said in frustration.

Deveraux and Langstrom had made their way, with the aid of several guards, back to the upper chamber where the aliens resided.

"What's going to happen now?" asked Langstrom as the two aliens and the figure formerly known as Reichstein met in the middle of the floor.

"We will show you," said one of them in the all too familiar cold, emotionless tone.

Far above them in the darkness of the chamber ceiling, a pale purple light flickered into being. Deveraux, forgetting about his injured leg tried to stand under his own weight as he looked up but winched and nearly fell had not one of the guards steadied him.

From within the light in the center of the ceiling, they saw the faint suggestion of tendrils whipping erratically back and forth and as the light grew; they saw what Ernst could only assume was a sort of giant jellyfish slowly descending from a darkened recess above them.

Without warning, the purple tendrils shot out in all directions and attached themselves to the three architects and to the heads of Langstrom and Deveraux. One of the guards cried inarticulately at this and ran from the chamber.

The other stood there and supported Deveraux. He would have run too but the tendril attached to the back of Deveraux's head had extended and entwined itself around the guard's wrist and he was powerless to move.

The giant, pulsating blob hovered a foot or so above their heads and one by one the aliens and former-Reichstein put a hand to it and touched its dry yet gelatinous surface. The blob quivered slightly at the touch and the guard that was trapped with Deveraux was looking intently at it.

He fancied that he could make out a tiny pair of black eyes near the base and a sort of wedge-shaped mouth below them. It seemed to make no actions of its own but was merely the most primitive intelligence, here to serve its masters.

It had the appearance of a cross between a giant translucent puffer fish and a grossly distended insect. He felt queasy but couldn't help but look at it as it pulsed and quivered.

Deveraux and Langstrom both stood stock still, a glazed expression on both their faces as the tendrils pulsed around their heads, and Deveraux was mumbling to himself in a faint voice, "No, you can't," over and over again.

The creature suddenly convulsed and released the tendrils from around Deveraux's and Langstrom's heads as the aliens removed their hands from its underside, and it drifted silently back up into the roof cavity.

"You see, we will make life better for all mankind," said one of the figures as Langstrom shook his head and wiped his hand across his face.

Deveraux was still in a kind of trance, but the guard, attempting to leave now that his hand was free, moved away and Deveraux fell to the ground with a thump.

He rapidly recovered from his torpor.

"OVER MA DEAD BODY!" he shouted, and still sitting on the ground reached for his pistol, but before he could extend his arm into the firing position, the pistol shot from his grip and flew into the hand of the former Reichstein.

"That would not be very wise, Mr. Deveraux," it hissed.

Its eyes blazed with an inhuman, blue intensity.

"Got it!" said Neville as he finally managed to dislodge the ruby skull from its mount.

"Right, let's see if we can get this thing to give up its secrets," said Madeline excitedly.

They both stood in front of the Cerebratome with the skull.

"Which socket?" asked Neville as Madeline scanned her notes.

"Try this one," she said, pointing to the third socket to the right of them.

Neville carefully placed the skull in the socket and stood back. Nothing happened.

"Maybe it has to be placed in the mirror image of this socket," said Neville as he removed the skull and walked around to the opposite socket.

"Well, anything's worth a try; it's not as if we're stuck for options," said Madeline as she followed him. Neville stood before the socket with the four stripe crescent moon symbol below and the symbol that looked like a tidal wave above. He stretched out his hands to place the skull in the socket, but before he had got it less than two inches away, it was sucked from his hands and the skull clicked into place. There was a low buzzing sound, and the top dais of the Cerebratome slowly started to rotate until the wave symbol was on the opposite side.

The symbol that was now above the ruby skull bore a striking resemblance to a flame, and with a grinding clunk, a section of the dais above the socket opened and a golden rod extended and curved up towards the center.

As Madeline and Neville watched in awe, the rod locked into place amid the intricate device that surmounted the top tier, and the skull lit up with a fiery red glow and the jaw dropped open, revealing a small silver sphere.

"Now let's switch it off," said Madeline, but as she attempted to remove the skull, a bolt of red electricity struck her hand and made her jump back with surprise and fear.

"Good god! Are you alright?" asked Neville. Madeline nodded but looked a little shaken.

Neville picked up the metal clamp and attempted to dislodge the skull with it but met with no success.

On his last attempt, he lost his grip on the clamp and it fell from his hand, but as it did so, the clamp pinged upwards and snapped the skull's jaw shut.

The red glow faded and the golden rod slid back into place.

The Cerebratome sat before them, lifeless once more.

"Just like an on and off switch!" chuckled Neville. He removed the skull from its socket and wrapped it up in Madeline's white coat for safe keeping.

Suddenly, the elevator motor whined into life the car was called back to the surface.

"I wonder which of the three stooges will be down to entertain us next?" said Neville, but they were in for a surprise, because when the car returned to the bottom of the shaft, out stepped Wilhelm Reichstein, but he didn't look at all well.

Chapter 19

The Origins of the Architects

"Have you made any progress?" asked Reichstein in an eerily flat tone.

Madeline and Neville could tell something was wrong. Reichstein was never this direct and it was this along with the unhealthy blue tint to his skin and eyes that made them very weary.

"Um no, not a sausage!" said Neville as convincingly as he could.

"We are becoming impatient," said Reichstein.

Madeleine cast Neville a knowing glance. "Where is Mr. Deveraux?" she asked.

"Deveraux is no concern of yours," it said with mechanical clarity. "We are not accustomed to being trifled with," said Reichstein.

"How are you coping with only two arms now?" asked Neville.

Reichstein looked down at the two, thin gangly arms. "They will suffice for now," said the inhuman, cold voice.

"Ah, thought as much—you've possessed him haven't you? Please tell me, how do you accomplish this?" Neville said his eyes full of wonder.

"We don't have time for science lessons!" whispered Madeline.

"On the contrary. I will tell you if you can tell me what you have discovered about the device," said Reichstein.

Neville walked over to the Cerebratome and leaned on it, arms outstretched. "You first," he said dryly.

Reichstein stared at them both for a few moments with those eerie blue eyes. "Very well." he said.

"We are the remains of an ancient race known as the Alubaantuni. Our species originates from what you refer to as the Andromeda galaxy, but ten thousand years ago, a vanguard took up an observational position on your fourth planet to oversee the development of man. We saw you as a potential threat."

Madeline was rapidly linking all the last few hundred years of alien related history to these creatures that were now with them in this complex. Reichstein continued.

"We came to your Earth some eight thousand years ago and entrusted the skulls to the safe keeping of a highly advanced civilization that resided on a remote island in your Atlantic ocean, but they betrayed us and attempted to utilize the power of the skulls to their owns ends, so they were erased and the skulls were moved to this mountain range."

Neville instantly recognized the abbreviated name of the aliens spelled the word *Lubaantun*, the name of the ancient city whose legendary ruins sat atop the plateau where Belinda had been digging.

"Twenty of our kind remained behind to guarantee the safety of the skulls, but there are others who still wish to obtain the skulls for their own malignant uses."

Neville began to think that his original hypothesis had some merit after all. "Did these ancient people worship you at all?" he asked.

"Yes. For a long time we were revered as gods, and effigies were erected in worship," answered Reichstein dryly.

"That explains Easter Island!" whispered Neville as he stood up and stretched his arms.

"Let me get this straight. You've been here for eight thousand years. You set up a base on Mars to spy on us, came to earth and set up numerous other observation posts, and then gave us the skulls to look after. Am I right so far?"

Reichstein just stared at him with those eerie blue eyes. "Yes," he finally said.

"So if you have been here for this long, has the process of regeneration caused a loss in memory?" Reichstein just stared.

"Because the only thing that bothers me, is why do you need our help to unlock something that YOU claim to have created!"

Madeline didn't feel very comfortable as Reichstein took a step towards them.

"Do you mean to question us?" asked Reichstein.

Neville was about to answer when Reichstein raised a hand, and Neville began wheezing and clawing at his throat.

"No!" screamed Madeline. "Let him go!" she yelled. "I'll show you what we've found out! Please, just don't hurt him."

Reichstein lowered his hand and Neville fell to his knees, gasping desperately.

"You bloody idiot!" said Madeline as she bent down to help him up.

"You!" said Reichstein, glaring at Madeline. "Show me how you operate the device."

Madeline picked up the skull that was still wrapped in her coat. She gently unwrapped it and walked around to the third socket on the right had side and placed the skull in the socket. Nothing happened.

"Is this all you have discovered?" asked Reichstein, coldly.

"I'm afraid so. It's a very complex language, and we must have more time to study it," she said, her voice shaking slightly.

"I will consult with the others, and we will decide the fate of your associates. You have twelve hours," he said as he turned to leave via the elevator car.

When he had gone, Madeline ran to Neville. "We have to get

Deveraux, Langstrom and the others down here!" she said. "It's all about stopping these creatures now. I'm sure of it!"

Neville was inclined to agree with her, and they too, with the ruby skull in hand, ascended the lift shaft to find the others.

Upon reaching the main cavern floor, Neville observed that the utter chaos he had walked into some hours before was now replaced by an eerie calm.

A few people in white coats and some guards were milling about near one of the examination chambers, but besides them, there was no one about.

"What on earth has been going on up here?" exclaimed Madeline.

"I'm not entirely sure, but it's a lot better than it was a few hours ago, I can assure you!" replied Neville as he nervously looked around.

They both hurried around the perimeter of the cavern as Neville had done before and ended up at the cabin where Karl, Belinda and Tito were imprisoned. "Wait here, down here by this crate," said Neville as he darted off the find something to bust open the door.

Madeline crouched down by the crate as Neville headed over to one of the trucks. Inside the trailer, he found a veritable arsenal of weaponry and excavation equipment, but being slightly naive as to the power of some weapons, he picked up what he took to be some sort of battering ram.

A few minutes later, he met Madeleine at the crate and they darted back to the cabin where Neville rapped hard on the thick glass to get their attention.

Tito's face appeared at the window and he smiled when he saw Madeline and Neville standing there, but his smile turned to horror when Neville held up the long steel tube, smiled and pointed at the door.

As Neville and Madeline ran around to the door they failed to notice Tito frantically waving his arms and shaking his head.

"Get back!" shouted Tito.

Karl almost jumped out of his skin as Tito pulled one of the bunks over and dove behind it, shielding himself with the two mattresses.

Belinda and Karl looked on in amazement as Tito stuck his head out from the makeshift bunker and told them what Neville was intending to do.

Karl and Belinda looked at each other, and in unison, dove under the mattresses with Tito.

Outside, Madeline watched as Neville attempted to activate the "ram."

He followed the instructions and pulled back the sheathe exposing a handle and trigger.

"Um, Neville, is this a wise idea?" she said nervously.

"Of course, we need to free them somehow, and this battering ram should do the trick nicely!" he said as he held the bazooka upside down by the handle, roughly aimed at the door, which was less than ten feet away, and squeezed the trigger.

There was a fizzing sound and a small green rocket ejected from the tube in a cloud of smoke. Neville was thrown backwards and they watched as the rocket hit the door of the cabin and obliterated it to matchwood and twisted metal, along with half the wall.

As the smoke cleared, Neville and Madeline rushed over to what remained of the front wall and saw the last remains of the nearest bunk crumple into smoldering ruins.

"What have I done?" declared Neville. "I thought it was a battering ram!" he said with tears welling up in his eyes, but Madeline gripped his arm as she saw the smoking mattresses move and topple off of the three coughing and spluttering inmates who had, until now, frequented an almost impregnable prison.

"Bloody good show, old boy!" said Karl as he attempted to stand up and nearly fell over again, slightly shell shocked.

"Quick, they'll be coming soon!" said Madeline as she ushered the three of them out of the remains of the cabin and across the cavern floor to hide amid the machinery near the regenerators as they saw a group of guards and scientists flock around the twisted hulk of the cabin.

"We must help Deveraux and Langstrom and get hold of the other skulls!" said Neville quietly.

"Have you gone potty, old bean?" said Karl as he plucked splinters of wood from his hair.

Hidden amid the bulk of the machinery, Madeline and Neville told them what they had learned and pressed upon them a severe urgency to help put a stop to whatever the aliens where planning.

Up in the main chamber, Langstrom and Deveraux were seated by the entrance while one of the aliens was busy with something over in a darkened corner.

"Why must you commit yourselves to such a futile endeavor?" asked the alien closest to them.

Langstrom looked up. "You're talking about assimilating the entire population of the planet!" he said, his voice shaking with anger and fear.

"You have abused this world, and now you want to destroy anything that can offer it a new lease of life?" said the alien in a droll, monotone voice.

Deveraux spat on the ground. "You'll rue the day you ever locked horns with Marcus Eugene Deveraux, you slimy freak!"

The alien looked at him curiously with its tiny eyes. "I am still attempting to grasp the concept of your fruitless attempts at intimidation, Mr. Deveraux," it said. "You truly are a barbaric species, aren't you?"

Deveraux laughed. "Do I detect an insult? You're no different from us. Ah'd wager you strip-mined your own planet and that's why you want ours!" he said viciously.

"Silence!" said the Alubaantuni, its voice slightly raised.

"You really are the worst cotton-pickin' liar I ever did see!" retorted Deveraux.

The other alien came back to the center of the room as former-Reichstein entered. "We have located the final skull," said the Alubaantuni, and it raised its thin hand and a guard walked in. "Take a squad and recover the final skull from these coordinates," it said.

With the ease of a telepathic transfer, the guard stood there with a blank expression on his face before nodding and leaving the chamber.

"Soon our plan will be complete, and we will once more rejoin our brothers among the stars," said former-Reichstein.

"Ya know, ah kinda like this fellow better than the old Wilhelm Reichstein, but I can't believe that little worm was right all along!" whispered Deveraux.

Former-Reichstein convened with the other two aliens in the center of the chamber and Deveraux saw his chance.

"Ah think now is as good a time as any to make our exit, Langstrom," he said in hoarse whisper.

"I agree," said Ernst as they both sidled out of the chamber and down the steps, Langstrom shouldering Marcus as they descended.

As they rounded the edge of the cavern, they saw a small group of people running from cabin to cabin with what appeared to be black haversacks loaded with something rather heavy.

"Who's that?" inquired Deveraux as they hobbled a bit faster to put as much distance between them and the chamber.

"I'm not sure," answered Langstrom. The two rested for a moment behind an outcrop of rock.

"What in the world have we done, agreeing to help these bastards!" said Marcus, panting heavily.

"I suppose that the only thing left to do is to try and right the wrongs we've committed," said Langstrom mournfully.

"Just as long as I get to keep that money, I'll be as happy as a pig in shi—"

Deveraux didn't finish the sentence because Langstrom was glaring at him, his mustache twitching angrily.

After ransacking the cabins, Tito, Belinda, Neville, Karl and Madeline headed back to the elevator shaft. But as they approached, they say the bulky figures of Deveraux and Langstrom hurriedly racing for it as well.

They all ran, but seemed to reach the car at the same time and they stood at the car, staring at each other, Karl and Deveraux both panting heavily.

"So, your little plan backfired, eh, Marcus?" snorted Karl.

Tito elbowed him in the side. "Now's is nota the time for bickering!" he said.

"I am truly sorry for this, all of you," said Ernst as he adjusted his grip on Marcus.

"I hope we can put aside our differences, at least until this whole nasty business is over."

Belinda looked at the others. They all seemed to agree except Karl. "Works for me!" she said as they all crammed into the elevator car.

"If you try anything, Deveraux, I will not be held responsible for my actions."

Deveraux glowered at him. "Watcha gonna do, slap me with your checkbook?" he replied.

The two Alubaantuni and former-Reichstein entered the cavern from their chamber and stood surveying the scene. People were beginning to realize that something was amiss, and they were frantically trying to secure a way out of the cavern. On by one, the Alubaantuni and Reichstein raised their hands, and people were stopping in their tracks and clutching at their throats and chests. One or two technicians and guards clambered aboard the wedge in a vane attempt to try and fly it to safety, but with a slight hand gesture from Reichstein, the wedge began smoking at the sides and windows when it suddenly went up in a conflagration of red and blue flames.

Others were trying to escape via the transporter trucks, but they were trying to drive and free the invisible crushing force at their throats at the same time, which resulted in them mowing down numerous people in the attempt.

Machinery exploded and chunks of rock fell from the ceiling, crushing the terrified people who ran this way and that.

After no more than five minutes, there was nothing but total destruction to be seen on the cavern floor.

Down in the chamber, they all filed out of the elevator and surrounded the Cerebratome.

"Any luck?" inquired Ernst.

Neville looked at him with suspicious eyes. "What did you mean earlier when you said 'this nasty business'?" asked Neville.

Ernst propped Marcus against the Cerebratome, mopped his brow and proceeded to tell them that he and Marcus had been subjected to a mind surge, and they now knew exactly what the Alubaantuni were intending to do with the Cerebratome.

"You see, this device has the ability to impart vast amounts of knowledge and possesses the power to create entire worlds, but in the wrong hands, it can absorb vast amounts of energy and be used as a weapon to destroy them. It can also be used as a portal, and that's what they want it for."

Karl gasped and Belinda clapped her hand over her mouth.

"If I am correct in reciting the information that I have ascertained, the Cerebratome was created millennia ago by a race called the Ortecs. They intended it as a library for the cumulative knowledge of their civilization and wanted to share it with other races in the universe as they felt that they had reached the peak of evolutionary perfection."

Madeline stared at the Cerebratome. It seemed hard to believe what appeared to be a lifeless chunk of stone could destroy entire worlds.

Deveraux continued the narration. "These lanky freaks are nothin' more than a scoutin' party waitin' for us saps to uncover it. They couldn't let themselves be seen 'cause there's still an Ortec descendant here today! Thing is, they don't know who it is!"

Belinda stood there with a look of total amazement on her face. "But why do they want destroy earth?" she said in a hushed voice.

Langstrom looked at all of them as they stood around the Cerebratome "They don't want to destroy it, they want to use it as a base of operations to assume control of the galaxy," he said.

"Until now, none of us had understood the true gravity of the situation, but they no longer consider us to be a threat and so intend to assimilate us into their race, just as Reichstein has been assimilated."

Madeline offered a conjecture. "Are we to assume that when they die, they become pure energy, seeking a new host to inhabit?"

"Damn, girl! You're pretty smart for a filly!" Deveraux chuckled. "We gotta stop 'em! If they activate the Cerebratome, they'll be able to open a gateway to their own world and let the rest o' them varmints through!"

Karl shot Deveraux a cold stare. "And you think that because you are now attempting to save the world that makes everything okay?"

Deveraux spat on the ground. "You don't like me, an' Ah don't like you, but you're gonna have to face it, Bub—we're partners again!" He grinned with his tobacco stained teeth.

Neville ripped open the bags. "Right, no more wasting time. Quickly, take the skulls!" he said.

Neville and Belinda handed a skull to each of them. Karl received the topaz and copper colored skulls, Tito, the white onyx and bronze skulls, Belinda the ruby and silver skulls, Deveraux, the emerald and gold skulls, Langstrom the jade and beryl skulls, and Madeline the bauxite skull.

Neville picked up the crystal skull, and each of them in turn followed Madeline and Neville's instructions on where to stand. One by one, the skulls were sucked from their hands and clicked into place.

The golden rods slid out from their concealed casings and met in the center, but suddenly they then realized that they were missing a skull.

"Shit, what now?" said Deveraux.

There was the clunk of a metal gate behind them, and they all turned to see four guards, the two Alubaantuni and Reichstein step out of the elevator car.

"Now, the plan comes to fruition!" said Reichstein. As they approached, Deveraux and the others saw that he carried in his hands the thirteenth skull, a skull of blackest jet.

Chapter 20
The Beginning of the End?

The guards, all wearing blank expressions, leveled their weapons and ushered Neville and the others away from the Cerebratome.

"Thank you for your assistance, Mr. Deveraux and associates," said former-Reichstein as he approached the Cerebratome.

"Now begins a new world for you and all your brethren," he said.

He let go of the last skull as it sucked from his hands and clicked into place.

One by one, the jaws of the skulls dropped open and a light issued forth from the eye sockets.

The last golden rod slid into place and the central mechanism began to spin wildly. Multicolored electrical light cascaded in crackling arcs down the rods as the upper and lower daises began to spin slowly in opposite directions.

Deveraux cursed silently to himself.

"What have we done?" said Neville as they all watched in disbelief from their guarded position.

Slowly, an image started to form in the swirling multicolored vortex at the center of the mechanism, and with a grinding crunch, the dais stopped dead. The image burst forth like a holographic firework and filled the chamber with a shifting, rippling image of the universe, and an enormous visual map of the galaxies, quasars and nebulae that made up the known universe.

Karl watched wide eyed as a tiny rendition of the crab nebula drifted past his left cheek. He curiously touched the image, and in a flash, the image had enlarged to focus on the nebula.

Thousands of inhabited worlds sprang up on smoky charts that hung in the air around them, and Neville watched in utter disbelief as one by one, images of various alien life forms were displayed with information in a weird, unreadable language. Every planet the Ortecs had visited had been logged and entered onto this miraculous device.

Reichstein and the other two Alubaantuni gathered around the Cerebratome and one by one, they collected the tiny silver spheres from the jaws of the skulls.

Deveraux was the first to notice the fact that the guard's eyes were unmoving, cold and staring, and what made him more curious was the fact that none of them blinked.

"Ah think we're being toyed with, Langstrom!" he whispered and with that, he struggled to his feet using the wall for support.

The guards didn't move. Deveraux waved a hand in front of their faces. No reaction. Karl saw what he was doing and did the same with the guard nearest him and this time, he tried to dislodge the gun from the guard's hand, but it was stuck fast.

"Zombies!" he declared in a hushed tone.

Karl turned to Belinda and Neville, but stopped and stared wide eyed at Tito.

Belinda saw that he was gawping at something and looked at Tito as well.

"Tito, your pendant!" she said.

Neville, Langstrom and Madeline also looked at Tito's chest.

From beneath the fabric of his shirt, the pendant was glowing brightly with a golden hue.

"Tito?" said Belinda as she griped his arm, but Tito seemed not to hear her. He stood up and serenely walked past the guards towards the Cerebratome.

"What in tarnation?" declared Deveraux as he watched the tall Mexican stride slowly towards Reichstein and the two Alubaantuni busy around the Cerebratome.

He stopped a few feet from them and pulled the pendant from around his neck and clasped it in his fist. "Noquaku carjamarka," he said in a deep, bellowing voice that was definitely not Tito's.

Belinda and the others looked on, awestruck by the spectacle.

Former-Reichstein turned around and saw that Tito was standing before them.

"He speaks the language of the creators. It appears that we have found the Ortec descendant."

Tito opened his hand and the light from the pendant narrowed into a tight beam and struck the spinning vortex atop the Cerebratome. The spinning mechanism slowed and suddenly stopped, and the misty image of the universe winked out like a dead light bulb, leaving a loud crackling residual charge sparking around the chamber.

The brightest light in the otherwise darkened chamber was the faint blue glow from the Alubaantuni and the golden aura that now surrounded Tito.

One of the Alubaantuni raised his hand, and the guards spun around to face Tito.

Deveraux, who was still holding onto one of them, let go and lost his grip and fell onto his bad leg. He yelped with pain as he tried to get up again.

With a mental order from one of the aliens, the guards opened fire and a hale of bullets showered Tito, but some of the bullets burnt up in a flash upon hitting him, while others ricocheted off into other parts of the chamber.

Karl squealed as a bullet entered the earth near to where he sat, and Belinda, realizing, that they were dangerously exposed, ushered them over to the elevator motor. They all darted for cover behind the big red metal casing while Karl, seeing that Deveraux was struggling, went back and heaved the big man up with his shoulder and hobbled as fast as they could to the safety of cover with the others.

Tito moved his hand so that the beam now pointed at the first Alubaantuni's head. A pulse of gold light shot forth and struck him squarely in the face, and a second later, he crumpled into a heap on the floor. The same earsplitting screech was heard, but this time, instead of forming a ball of crackling blue light, the vapor issuing from the body of the fallen alien seemed to crackle spasmodically before popping and hissing into nothingness.

Reichstein, forgoing the usual placid manner of the Alubaantuni, launched himself at Tito with hands like claws outstretched.

He struck with full force, and the two men rolled to the ground while the pendant shot out of Tito's hand into the air. Reichstein rolled off of him and quickly jumped up to snatch the pendant.

"Now you will pay for your insolence!" he hissed. Tito seemed lifeless as he lay on the ground at Reichstein's feet, but before anyone could stop him, Langstrom ran out from behind the motor housing and bolted straight for Reichstein.

He howled with rage as he charged headlong at him, but the guards were still in position, and just as the remaining Alubaantuni was raising his hand, a spanner flew out of nowhere and struck his fingers so hard that it caused him to scream an inhuman scream of pain.

"Good shot, Neville!" said Karl as Neville stood there, weighing up the projectile properties of a monkey wrench.

Karl, Madeline and Belinda saw their opportunity and darted out to the line of guards. Karl grabbed the rifle of one, but it still wouldn't budge.

"Karl, ever played dominos?" shouted Belinda above the buzzing and crackling of the residual energy. Karl winked at her and rushed up to where she and Madeline stood.

They heaved all their weight behind the first guard in the line and he finally toppled, and as Belinda watched, they fell to the ground like lifeless mannequins. One of them lessened his hold on his weapon.

Madeline spotted this and snatched it from the now-relaxing grip of the zombie guard.

Langstrom grabbed Reichstein from behind, but no sooner than he had made contact, he too was surrounded by crackling blue electricity. With a violent jolt he was flung across the chamber and struck the far wall with immense power before falling, limp to the ground, dead.

The remaining Alubaantuni staggered around to the front of the Cerebratome and restarted it. The central mechanism started up again with a high-pitched whine, and a small gold platform rose up from within from the rim where he stood.

This platform had a multitude of tiny recesses in it, and the Alubaantuni began to frantically place the silver spheres in a structured formation on the tray. As it set the last sphere in place, a bolt of multicolored light burst fourth from the central spinning mechanism and a tiny patch of blue crackling light appeared twenty feet away from it. This light expanded and grew until through its shimmering multicolored hues, a panoramic scene of a desolate world could be seen with black-blue skies coursing with lightning, and in the foreground the vague resemblance of a leafless tree stood, dead and withered.

The portal continued to expand until it reached some thirty feet across, and as the scene cleared, they could see thousands upon thousands of blue pulsating balls of light, similar to the one that had possessed Reichstein.

"Not on ma watch!" growled Deveraux. Ignoring the pain, he got up and charged as Langstrom had done at the last Alubaantuni.

It was so busy frantically trying to stabilize the portal that it failed to see Deveraux approaching. Deveraux grabbed it by the robes and spun it around to face him. As he did so, the hood fell back and he came face to face with this mysterious entity.

He stared at it for a moment and the sheer disgust was evident on his face.

"Deal's off!" he shouted, and with that, he shouldered the cloaked figure, and with a cry of pure hatred, thrust it through the portal into the balls of light. Neville dashed over to the Cerebratome and dislodged the silver spheres from the tray. The portal flickered, crackled and began to shrink. The Alubaantuni on the other side was desperately trying to get back, but as the portal was closing, all that managed to poke through was an arm.

With a sickening slicing sound accompanied by a bloodcurdling scream, the arm was severed, the portal disappeared and the smoking limb dropped to the floor of the chamber.

Reichstein had seen what had happened and spun around to face the now drained and sweating Deveraux.

"You!" it said with raw malice. "You will pay for this with your insignificant life!"

Reichstein stuck out both hands and made a strangulation gesture in the direction of Deveraux.

Deveraux began to wheeze and cough and claw at his throat and chest as he was slowly lifted into the air.

"Drop him!" shouted Madeline as she trained the gun on Reichstein, but he took no notice of her.

"PISHTAKU QUOSQUO WASIKUNATA UKUNIPTI!" cried the now vertical Tito, his eyes aflame with power.

Reichstein sneered at Deveraux and released his grip, allowing Marcus to fall to the ground, landing on his injured leg. "I will return for you, human" he said as he turned his attention to Tito.

"So, the great descendant of the Ortecs has finally shown himself!" said former-Reichstein, his eyes burning with blue fire. "The Alubaantuni have waited centuries to obtain the power of the skulls, and you, a mere man, think you can stop us?"

Tito said nothing. He just advanced a few paces and sat down, cross-legged on the floor in front of him. "You worship me, how very wise of you," said Reichstein with a sinister chuckle.

Tito closed his eyes, raised his palms skywards and began chanting three words over and over. "Markarsha Bakayuna orinipto."

Reichstein looked a little puzzled, but his attention was soon drawn the Cerebratome, which was beginning to shake violently.

Deveraux lay, slightly insensible, over on the far side of the chamber as the others bolted back to the safety of the motor housing. One by one, the skulls disengaged themselves from their sockets and floated over towards Tito.

Reichstein still held the pendant in his hand and he tried to fire a beam at Tito, but nothing happened. It just sat in the palm of his hand and glowed. In frustration, he thrust his hands out as he done to Deveraux, but it had no affect on Tito.

The faint golden aura returned around Tito as he sat on the ground. He slowly lowered his arms, still chanting the same three words in that eerie voice.

The skulls settled into a circle, gently spinning above his head. Reichstein howled with frustration as he lunged at Tito, but he was thrown back with awesome force by an arcing yellow bolt.

"What on earth is going on?" exclaimed Karl in a shaky voice.

"I think we are witnessing the last stand of two ancient races," said Neville, hardly able to contain his excitement.

Reichstein had enough of playing games. With one last howl of anger, frustration and pain, the blue pulsing light seeped out through Reichstein's nose, eyes and mouth, leaving the limp corpse of what was once Wilhelm Reichstein the slump to the floor. The ball of light shot at full speed towards Tito and ricocheted off him with a massive arc of lightning.

Slowly, a ball of golden yellow light formed above Tito and fused with the aura that was around him. The ring of skulls began to spin faster and faster as the blue ball shot again at full speed towards Tito. This time, the skulls intervened and the two balls of light were now captured in a floating spinning arena, crackling and arcing lightning off one another.

The spinning circle of skulls began to shrink in diameter as the blue ball tried to escape from the slowly diminishing arena.

As it was about to float free, the golden orb let out lashing tendrils of electricity and it dragged the blue sphere into it. The two balls began to fuse, and Karl fancied that he heard an almost human scream come from the fading blue orb.

With one last crackle of light, the blue ball was fused with the gold, and in a final cascading light show of sparks, arcing electrical tentacles and noise, the two orbs imploded with a series of fizzing bangs.

The spinning circle of skulls began to slow down from the center, slowly falling to the ground was Tito's pendant.

Tito, still evidently under the influence of a higher power, picked up the pendant, uttered the word *rimani*, and the skulls flew back into their respective sockets with resounding clicks.

The others came out from behind the motor housing and gingerly approached the Cerebratome.

They watched as Tito bent down and picked up the thirteen silver spheres and placed them in the gold tray in a formation that Neville instantly recognized as the constellation of Orion's belt.

The Cerebratome flickered into life once more and a new portal opened out on a lush, verdant landscape dotted with bizarre structures that looked as if carved of ivory.

A tangerine sky was the backdrop for strange, broad winged creatures that flew lazily through the air, and as they watched, a hazy figure approached the portal.

Chapter 21
Are We Not Alone?

Neville could hardly contain his excitement any longer. He and Madeline gingerly walked to within feet of the portal, but Tito put out his arm to stop them.

The portal shimmered and multicolored waves rippled across its surface, and as they watched, a figure stepped through.

This figure was nothing like the Alubaantuni; instead, it was dressed in fine gold and silver robes with a pair of white feathered wings that protruded from its back, and the slender neck supported a narrow, serpentine face and head.

The elongated nostrils, absence of a chin and the beak-like mouth gave the creature a half snake, half bird-like appearance.

Its eyes were rather large and pale green in color. Atop its head sat a majestic feathered headdress that was so brilliant that the air around it seemed to shimmer.

"Is it a bird?" quizzed Karl, but Belinda hushed him by nudging him in the ribs.

"I think you'll find that we are in the presence of an Ortec," she said.

As she spoke that last word, the Ortec looked at her as if it had heard its name.

It beckoned her to approach, and after a moment of hesitating, she did and took a few steps closer.

Standing in the gaze of this strange being, Belinda felt oddly tranquil.

Soon the others had joined her like children gathering around a magician.

The Ortec said nothing but outstretched a slender feathered finger and touched each of them on the forehead then it spoke.

Not through regular channels, but as if it was speaking directly to their souls.

It cast its benign gaze at Deveraux and then at the crumpled body of Langstrom.

A tear welled up in its eye.

"We never intended our device to bring such pain and suffering," it said with a soft feminine voice.

"We must destroy it before it can be used for evil as it very nearly was today."

Deveraux came to and saw the image before him.

"Dang, Ah musta really banged ma noggin!" he said as he tried to stand up.

Tito saw that he was struggling and headed over to help him. "Mighty kinda you," he said, but Tito didn't reply.

Upon reaching the portal, Deveraux was wide eyed at the sight of the Ortec and nearly fell from Tito's support. She stretched a slender arm and touched his forehead

"Ah! The capitalist," she said.

Deveraux frowned with a confused look on his face. Was he hearing things as well?

"For all your bravery and selfless acts, I thank you. Someday, I hope that your race will reach the level of serenity and peace that we have enjoyed for centuries."

Neville, not to be put out, asked, "Um, might I ask, who are you?"

The Ortec smiled at him. "I have many names, but on your world, centuries ago I was called Quetzalcoatl."

She took Belinda's hand and placed in her palm a pendant similar to Tito's. "A gift, for your selfless acts," she said as she handed each of them a pendant, each one slightly different in design and color, ranging from deepest azure blue to the brightest golden yellow.

Karl bit his to test its worth and shook it by his ear.

Marcus looked indignant as he had received nothing.

"Where's mine?" he said.

Quetzalcoatl looked at him. "I thought that as you were in this endeavor for capital gain, capital gain is what you would most like to receive."

She reached into a pouch that was slung around her waist and pulled forth a diamond the size of a potato.

"Will this suffice?" she asked as she handed it to him.

Deveraux's eyes nearly bulged out of his head. "Hot dog! That's the mother lode!" he said as he whistled, remarking at the purity of the crystal.

Karl nudged him with his elbow and Marcus seemed to get the idea.

"Uh, thanks missy, uh I mean quaza...quetz...oh dang!"

Quetzalcoatl tipped her head but then looked at all of them with a deadly serious expression.

"It is of the utmost importance that you never speak of the skulls, me or of the Alubaantuni."

She outstretched on arm and pointed to the Cerebratome.

"The device must be destroyed at all costs. Without it, the skulls are useless."

Belinda seemed to be in two minds as to whether to agree to this; after all they did contain the history of the universe and the secrets to eternal peace.

"Why not simply hide them as they were before?" she answered. "I mean it took the Alubaantuni nearly eight thousand years to find them, didn't it? And we could learn an awful lot from them," she added.

Quetzalcoatl lowered her head towards Belinda.

"If you feel that you can commit yourselves to safeguard the skulls, then so be it. This is your fate. You are now the guardians of the skulls."

She stepped back through the portal and raised a hand. Tito seemed to snap out of a trance, took one look at the scene before him and smiled as if saying goodbye to an old friend.

Deveraux, however, slipped from Tito's grip and collapsed on his still throbbing leg. He sat up with tears of pain in his eyes but that didn't stop him examining the truly massive diamond as he struggled to bite off the end and light his last fat Havana cigar.

The portal flickered, shimmered and disappeared with a faint *pop*, and the humming from the Cerebratome ceased as the light from the spinning mechanism faded and winked out.

"Well, that was fun!" exclaimed Karl with an air of sarcasm.

Neville was busy examining the Cerebratome when Karl came waddling over.

"What do you make of this now, old bean. Real aliens, eh?"

Neville was elated at finding what he'd been searching all his life for.

"I still can't believe its real!" he said with a slightly shaking voice as he ran over to the severed alien arm that still lay on the floor. "Look! I'd like to see those skeptics back at the institute make fun of me now!" he said, but as he spoke, the severed arm began to decompose and crumble in his hands. "Oh bugger!" he said, stamping his foot.

"We'd better get out of here. I need some air!" said Belinda. Tito agreed.

"I can't help but feel sorry for poor Langstrom" said Madeline as they looked at his crumpled and broken body, still lying in the corner of the chamber. Tito laid a hand on her shoulder.

"Don't worry, we'll give him a good burial," he said as he smiled at her.

They were about to ascend the shaft in the elevator car when Neville spotted Karl fiddling with the Cerebratome.

"I wouldn't touch that If I were you, Karl," he said but it was too late.

Karl's curiosity had gotten the better of him, and he had been fiddling with the central mechanism. He accidentally pulled free one of the small, intricately etched golden gyroscopes and the Cerebratome made a worrisome whining noise.

Suddenly, Karl jumped back and ran over to the others, entering the elevator car as shafts of light shot out from the skulls and the Cerebratome shuddered violently.

"Weston! Get in here!" Deveraux shouted from the elevator car.

The chamber began to shake and pieces of the ceiling began to fall in great chunks. The guards, no longer under the control of the Alubaantuni came to with a fright.

Dazed and confused in a chamber that was collapsing around them, they spotted the others in the elevator car and got up and ran to it. The last to enter was Karl, and it was a really tight squeeze, but he managed to close the metal gated as Deveraux threw the switch. As the ascended the shaft, they all saw the Cerebratome glowing and crackling wildly. They all felt the car shudder as the chamber below them collapsed in on itself.

Eventually they reached the top and there was a mad dash to get out of the cavern, which was also cracking and falling to pieces around them. Suddenly, there was a horrific splitting noise and a rift opened in the floor, and Deveraux lost his footing.

He tripped up and slid down into the fissure, but managed to keep a grip with his one remaining hand. Karl, hearing his cries for help, rushed back and was nearly hit in the face as a large glittering object whizzed past his head.

"Help me!" cried Deveraux.

Karl bent down on the shifting and shaking ground and stretched out a hand. Deveraux took it, but he was a heavy man to say the least.

Karl heaved with all his might and managed to get Deveraux halfway out when a violent shock underfoot caused Deveraux to slip back.

"For god's sake, Karl! Pull me up!" he yelled.

Karl was not in the mood for vulgar conversation and heaved with all his might, and to his surprise, Deveraux came out of the fissure with ease this time.

"I must be stronger than I thought!" he said to himself, which was until he saw Tito standing next to him.

They were about to run when Deveraux pulled them back and bent down to collect the diamond he had thrown out of the fissure to free his other hand. Tito and Karl glowered at him.

They hurried out of the tunnel with Deveraux supported between them.

Outside, the rest of them had made it to a safe distance when Tito, Karl and the still incapacitated Deveraux joined them.

When they stopped, they deposited Deveraux on the ground, and Karl mopped his brow with a handkerchief. No one noticed Deveraux softly speaking into the concealed radio that he had unhooked from his belt

"Nice going, Karl!" said Belinda as they felt the rumbling beneath their feet subside.

"Well, look at it this way, no one will find any of that little lot for a long—"

He stopped short as they all looked up.

A loud explosion had ruptured the plateau that sat atop the cavern complex, and a massive bolt of bright gold energy shot skywards with such force that it caused a sonic boom, throwing several of them backwards as tiny particles of dust and grit showered them from above.

As they watched in the dying light of the day, the bolt of energy burst like a firework in the heavens. The remnants continued skywards while thirteen little flares shot off in all directions and faded into the distant dusk.

"Well, that's that!" said Neville with a sigh.

Madeline looked sternly at Deveraux. "Now tell me, where's my father?"

Deveraux looked at her. He knew his game was up and that it was pointless to keep lying to the poor woman. "He was last heard of six months ago. Apparently heading for Iceland," he finally said.

She couldn't stay angry at Deveraux after all that had just happened. Yes, he had called her bluff and she had fallen for it, but she was exhausted.

A single tear of happiness trickled down her cheek; her father was alive.

Belinda looked at Tito.

"You've got a hell of a lot of explaining to do!" she said with an inquisitive smile.

"One question," said Karl. "How on earth are we going to get back to civilization?"

As he spoke, the familiar sound of a helicopter was audible, and within minutes, it had landed and they saw Deveraux hobbling hurriedly towards it accompanied by the guards.

Before any of them realized what was going on, Deveraux was in the helicopter and was lifting off the ground

"Deveraux, you bastard!" shouted Belinda.

Deveraux smiled at them and slid back the window panel and dropped the radio down to them

"Don't say I never do anything for ya!" he said with a laugh as the helicopter rose into the air and flew off across the plain.

Tito caught the radio, and after adjusting the frequency, he managed to contact a local authority for help.

Deveraux was laughing to himself in the co-pilot seat as he admired the huge diamond before him but as he watched, the diamond grew dull, then opaque and finally white before crumbling into dust that fell between his fat, nicotine stained fingers, and he cursed and swore for all he was worth.

Two hours later, Karl and the others were flying over the Peruvian plains in the direction of Lima, Peru's capital city. They knew that Marcus Deveraux was long gone and would not be caught easily, but they had time, plenty of time.

The energy pulse that had been released by the Cerebratome, shot out of the solar system and was charging its way through the cosmos when it passed something, something of vast intelligence that had until now paid very little attention to the lesser, younger beings of the universe. But slowly it turned it's attention to the third tiny blue planet orbiting an ordinary star near the outer rim of the Milky Way Galaxy, and it was curious.

Epilogue

The thirteen tiny stars radiating from the energy burst witnessed by the group up on the remote plateau fell to earth some hours later. Many fell back to earth around the South American continent and equatorial regions, but several shot much farther.

One skull was expelled with such force that it made its way through the atmosphere so fast that within two hours it had landed in the remote highlands of Scotland.

Many people must have seen the fall, but had taken it to be nothing more than a common falling star.

Some months later, as life returned to normal for the now fragmented group, Karl Weston had gotten a real taste for archeology and had subsequently funded further digs in South America, and had also founded the Weston-Osborne institute of archeology in California, but he returned to England some months later to resume his leisurely days at the Connaught club for wealthy gentry in his home town of Winchester.

Marcus went under his middle name of Eugene for a while to evade the authorities and later, set up an illegal oil trafficking racket in Texas where he spent his ill-gotten gains and his spare time at his ranch.

Neville and Madeline had returned to the United States together and both managed to get research positions with SETI in Pasadena.

They were both working late one night at the observatory when two very strange events occurred.

As they were monitoring a radio frequency feedback from deep space, Neville noticed that the pendant around his neck was giving off a faint glow.

He pointed this out to Madeline, who looked down at her own pendant and noticed that hers too was giving off a faint light.

Seconds later, the detection monitoring system designed to pick up intelligent signals from deep space went berserk and lit the up the screen like a Christmas tree.

They both saw that a radio energy pulse was being produced by something very strong and very large.

What concerned them was that the signal intervals were getting shorter, indicating that whatever was producing them was getting nearer.

Tito and Belinda ended up taking a field trip from the institute to Scotland where they were excavating the ruins of an ancient king's burial site.

Not far from this site, on the outskirts of a remote village, a young boy was playing "diggers" with his friends when he stumbled across what they called "buried treasure."

The other boys insisted upon sharing it, but the term *finders, keepers* came into play and he rushed home to hide his booty.

He reached his home and ran in through the kitchen door, starling his mother and splattering mud all over the floor.

His father, a tall scholarly man, was in his study smoking a calabash pipe charged with sweet cherry tobacco and reading a slim volume when his son came bounding in, sweating and covered in mud.

"Da, Da! Look what Ah foond!" exclaimed the boy.

His father lowered the book and peered over the top of his glasses, but the book fell from his hands when he saw what his son was holding.

Dirty, caked in mud and grit, but still clearly visible was a skull, a skull of purest jade.

Printed in the United Kingdom
by Lightning Source UK Ltd.
105634UKS00001B/77